WHEN
DINOSAURS RULED
THE BASEMENT

WHEN
DINOSAURS RULED
THE BASEMENT

WILLIAM L. DeANDREA
and MATTHEW DeANDREA

AN AVON CAMELOT BOOK

WHEN DINOSAURS RULED THE BASEMENT is an original publication of Avon Books. This work has never before appeared in book form.

AVON BOOKS
A division of
The Hearst Corporation
1350 Avenue of the Americas
New York, New York 10019

First Avon Camelot Printing: December 1995

CAMELOT TRADEMARK REG. U.S. PAT. OFF. AND IN OTHER COUNTRIES, MARCA REGISTRADA, HECHO EN U.S.A.

Printed in the U.S.A.

OPM 10 9 8 7 6 5 4 3 2 1

To Gregory James DeAndrea, also known as the Nibblosaurus, and his mother

"If you see a stegosaurus in the kitchen," my little brother said, "*don't panic.* Just call me."

It was a Wednesday night in the middle of January. The three of us were in the TV room watching a tape of *The Absent-Minded Professor,* a film my brother Michael likes even though it's in black and white.

He likes it because of all the crazy stuff in it, like flying cars and shoes that can bounce you higher than a skyscraper. I like it because of the basketball game at the end. Not that there was ever a basketball game like that, or ever could be. It was just nice to see Michael exposed to something a little closer to normal than his usual tastes.

Michael is seven—I'm five years older. Brothers are supposed to bicker and fight, but we don't. Much. I suppose the fact that we don't have to share a room has a lot to do with it. That way, we don't run the risk of my breaking one of his dinosaur models, or of his getting monster goop on my sports posters.

My name is Jonathan, Jonathan Parlo. Please call me Jon.

See, that's one of the differences between us right there. If your name's Jonathan, the only possible nickname is Jon, the most common and boring name on the face of the earth. But look at the nicknames possible from Michael: Mike, Mick, Mickey, Mikey—good, tough, hard-hitting names.

So what does my brother want people to call him?

Michael. No nicknames, please.

Also, though my mom and the teachers at school and Mr. Weathersfield, the school superintendent, get all whispery about it, and try to keep it a secret, Michael is a genius.

I do okay in school and everything, but I'm no genius. I am, though, smart enough to realize that a seven-year-old who can help his seventh-grade brother in geometry and English grammar just might have a little more than usual on the ball.

Michael, amazingly enough, *doesn't* seem to realize it. I think he thinks that we normal people are acting dumb to tease him.

Aside from his brainpower, he's a normal enough little kid. He loves dinosaurs and monsters and super-heroes, and he cries if he thinks the good guy's about to get killed, and he laughs at himself when he realizes the hero knew how to spring himself from danger all the time.

I guess the only thing more remarkable about him than his brain is his imagination. He talks a lot, but sometimes he gets real quiet, and then we know he's off in a world of his own somewhere. Then he comes out and says something.

One night, in the middle of dinner, he came out with, "Slain are those who draw near!"

Since he dumped that into a conversation Mom and I were having about whether she'd be able to make it to Sports Night at the end of the basketball season, it kind of confused us for a minute. Michael explained that he was imagining a story about Slarn, metal-eating monster from the planet Taros. He was about four years old at the time.

So by the time he came up with the dinosaur remark, we were pretty well used to him. I just kind of smiled and shook my head, and Mom, without looking up from her paperwork, said, "All right, dear, I will."

Michael said, "Good," and sealed it with a nod. Then he went back to the movie.

Mom has almost always got paperwork to do. She's a lawyer, and she's always reading over contracts and wills and affidavits and all sorts of things. It's part of the deal we have. She spends as much time with us as possible—she has an arrangement with her partner, Judy Levitt, that lets her leave the office early three days a week. The other two days, we spend a couple of hours at Gemma Davis's house, and her mom and dad look after us. In return, Michael and I have to make it possible for her to work at home. We have our assigned chores, and mostly, we're glad to do them.

She's not unreasonable about it. She can work through practically any TV show, and she'll interrupt herself to talk to us. We can't play loud music, though, or fight.

That Wednesday evening was kind of a special night. When Michael gave Mom the stegosaurus warning, it was already past his bedtime and closing in on mine. The reason we were still up was that it was snowing again.

We moved to Marsdentown from the city after my dad died, about four years ago. Mom says it's the perfect place to raise kids—low crime, good schools,

3

friendly people, a healthy economy, and some of the best autumn leaves to be seen in all of the United States. It also had nice, cold winters, but it had been lacking a little in the snow department.

Until this year.

Actually, until this *month*. It had begun right after the end of winter vacation, all kinds of it. Little gritty ice crystals blown by winds until they scoured your face. Big storms that seemed to dump two inches of snow in half an hour, then vanish completely, leaving behind a sky so blue it hurt your eyes to look at it.

This time, it was still and quiet, though the snow-flakes fell in clumps so thick you expected them to go *whump!* when they landed.

The snow had already piled up past the first step of the porch, and there was no end in sight. It looked like another snow day off from school coming up.

Mom could see it, too. That's why she let us stay up.

Finally, the tape was over. I got up off the floor, stopped it and put it on rewind, and hit the switches so Mom could watch regular TV or cable after we went to bed.

She looked up from her papers. "Movie over? Then it's bedtime, guys."

Michael said, "Aw, Mom," and I made a face, but only because parents expect a reaction like that. If you admit you actually are tired and would just as soon go to sleep, they start wanting to take your temperature.

"There probably won't be any school tomorrow, any-way," I said, playing my part.

"Maybe not," she said. "Jon, you set your alarm for six o'clock and check the Allenbury radio station for school closings. Then leave me a note. If school's off,

4

and the roads are very bad, I may just stay home my-self tomorrow.''

"All *right!*" Michael said. "Want to come sledding with us?''

Mom laughed. "If I stay home tomorrow, I'm going to do some housework. This place is a mess."

We told her it looked all right to us, but she laughed at that, too.

"You two," she told us, "are blind when it comes to messes. Besides, cleaning the house will give me a chance to look for my earring."

"What earring?" I asked.

"One of the gold stars your father gave me after you were born, Jon.''

"Oh, rats," I said. Mom was being brave about it, but I knew those earrings meant an awful lot to her. She only wears them on special occasions.

"Don't worry so much," she said. "It has to be in the house. I wore them at the dinner party I threw for some of my clients last week."

"We'll help you find it, Mom," Michael said.

"Well, keep your eyes open for it," she said. "Now, bed!"

She whipped off her glasses and kissed us both. "I'll be up to tuck you in later." She was talking to Michael when she said that—supposedly. I have my suspicions, though. I think she sneaks in while I'm asleep and tucks me in, too. Either that, or I'm a very neat sleeper.

Anyway, upstairs we went. I looked at *Sports Illustrated* while Michael brushed his teeth. We have our own rooms, but we share a bathroom. When he was done, I went in and took care of myself. Then, as I

5

always do, I stopped near his door to make sure he was okay. And tease him a little, too. Okay, I never said I was perfect.

"Good night, squirt," I told him. "Watch out for those stegosauruses."

And then a funny thing happened. Usually, when I throw a line like that at him, Michael says something like, "Ha, ha, very funny."

Tonight, he just said, very seriously, "Don't worry, I will. Good night, Jon."

I didn't know why, but his seriousness made me feel a little funny.

"Yeah," I said. "Good night."

I'd set my alarm for five minutes to six so I could find the station before the school closings were announced. You have to listen to school closings from the beginning, because they never do them in order, and if you tune in the middle and don't hear the name of your school, you have to stay awake and listen to twenty minutes of commercials for hemorrhoid creams and travel agencies before they start up again.

This time, though, we were right near the front—all classes at Marsdentown schools canceled today.

"Hooray!" I said quietly. It wasn't that I hated school or anything. I just hate fighting my way to the bus stop in the snow. And sliding around in the back of a big yellow tin can with no seatbelts while Tommy Upton's mother sweats her hair wet trying to keep the thing on the road is no fun, either. If that makes me a chicken, too bad. It's the way I am. I worry about things. Our friend Gemma Davis says I worry too much.

There was nothing to worry about this morning, though. I scribbled a note for Mom, stuck it to her door, and went back to bed.

I had some weird dreams.

In one of them, I was running fast, trying to get to

something or away from something, I couldn't tell which, and that alone was pretty scary.

What made it worse was that I couldn't see very well. Everything was gray and sort of foggy, except that it wasn't cool and wet on my face the way real fog is. It was dry and wispy, like spiderwebs.

Then (in the dream), I stopped running and collapsed, and soon, in that crazy way things happen in dreams, I was lying in my bed. I heard voices—harsh, angry voices—but I couldn't make out any words, no matter how hard I strained to hear. Somehow, I knew it was vitally important to make out what they had to say, but I just couldn't. I couldn't even tell who was talking, a man, a woman, or a kid. It could have been a parrot, for all I knew. The voices had that kind of squawk to them people get when they're really ticked off.

Then I heard this whining, roaring noise, like a jet plane had started up in the bedroom.

I sat bolt upright, my eyes wide open, going, "What? What? What?"

Then I looked around and saw my old familiar room, with my posters and books and my town Little League championship baseball trophy, and relaxed.

The sound that had startled me awake turned out to be the vacuum cleaner. There was another sound, too, a rumbling sound I couldn't place, but if it didn't worry Mom, I didn't see why it should worry me.

I got out of bed, padded to the door and opened it. There was Mom, dressed in a way we hardly ever saw her anymore, in jeans and sneakers and a big old sweatshirt from State University. We've got lots of State U. stuff. Mom and Dad both went there. It's where they met.

She was so involved in her work and the vacuum was making so much noise that she didn't notice I'd opened the door.

When I said, "Hi, Mom," she jumped, then looked at me and smiled. It almost came as a surprise to me, because since you see her every day, you can sometimes forget how nice looking your mom is.

"Hello, lazybones," she said. "Michael's been up for ages."

"The vacuum woke me up."

"That was more or less the plan," she said.

"Are you going to be home all day?"

"Uh-huh. I talked to Judy, and we decided that anybody who needs legal work from us can wait a day."

"That's great," I said.

"This house needs some catching up with, that's for sure."

I opened my mouth.

Mom pretended to scowl. "If you're going to say it looks okay to you, *don't.*"

"All right," I told her. "I won't say it."

"Good."

She'd shut the vacuum off so we could talk without yelling but there was still an unfamiliar rumble in the house.

"What's that noise?" I asked.

"The dishwasher," she said.

I didn't want to tell her it sounded funny to me. It was nice of her to do a chore we all knew was mine, so I didn't want to seem be complaining. I made a mental note to check it.

I got dressed and went downstairs. Michael was sitting at the breakfast table in the kitchen, reading. His project for the last few months now has been this dinosaur encyclopedia Mom got him for his birthday back in November. It's bigger and thicker than the phone book, with a skillion pictures in it, but lots of words, too, and my little brother was reading every one of them.

I was impressed. Sure, he skipped around sometimes to check on his favorites, but mostly he plowed on through with a serious look on his face, taking it all in.

When Mom had told me what she was getting him, I asked Mr. Lupus, the shop teacher, if I could build him a rack for it, so he could read the thing without pulling his back out every time he tried to hold it.

He had the book in the reading rack now and was using his hands to hold the bowl and spoon as he shoveled soggy shredded wheat into his mouth.

"Goog morgig," he said.

I told him not to talk with his mouth full.

He finished and swallowed. "Good morning," he said. "There sure is a lot of snow out there."

I looked out the window. There sure was. The snow had come up to the third step of the back porch. That seemed to be an average height. The wind had sculpted it in long curves so that there was a shallow area running from the detached garage to the side of the house where the cellar hatchway was. Really deep drifts stood over where the pine trees lined the creek at the edge of our property.

The sun was bright, and the snow was so new—not even a squirrel print anywhere on it—that it hurt my eyes to look at it too long. As I turned away, the phone rang.

"I'll get it!" I yelled, but over the vacuum and the dishwasher, I doubt Mom even heard it.

It was Gemma.

"Hi," she said. "This weather is really something, isn't it?"

"Sure is. We may not be getting much education, but we're having a lot of fun."

"Fun. That's what I called you about."

"Sure," I said. "Sledding today?"

"Cool," she said.

I gave her one of Michael's reactions. "Ha, ha," I said.

"What?" she said, then, "Oh, right. The Amazing Davis strikes again. I make jokes even when I don't know I'm doing it."

"When are you coming over?" I asked.

"Is half an hour okay? Mom's got the Jeep out delivering a printer. When she comes back, she'll run me over there. If it's okay, that is."

"Hold on a second."

I put the phone down and ran up to ask Mom. As I expected, she said it would be okay. She invited Gemma to stay for dinner. I heard her tell Mrs. Davis once that Gemma was a good influence on me. Whatever she meant by that. Makes me sound like a juvenile delinquent or something.

I went back downstairs and got everything all arranged. I passed along my mother's reminder for Gemma to bring along a change of clothes, which was good advice, because when we sled, we *sled*.

Gemma showed up all ready to go. She wore a bulky silver suit that covered her head to foot, black waterproof boots, and bright red mittens. Her hood was laced

11

down tight to her head, hiding her shortish carroty-red hair, and dark ski goggles hid her crinkly green eyes. All you could see of her was the tip of her nose and two cheeks, both covered with freckles, and her wide smiling mouth. Even her chin was covered by a bit of the yellow scarf that was buried under the ski suit. She held a red plastic snow saucer in one hand, and a plastic bag with her change of clothes in the other.

When I took the bag from her I would have laughed, except for three things. One, since I started seventh grade, I've noticed that people can get really upset when you talk about their clothes. In a lot of ways, Gemma is the most sensible kid I know, and she probably wouldn't take offense, but why take chances?

Two, I knew I was going to look equally silly as soon as I got into my stuff.

And three, you go sledding to have fun; you don't go sledding to show off how you *look*.

Of course, my brother, the genius, hasn't figured it out. As soon as Gemma walked through the door, he said, "Arrgghhh!" he said. "It's the Attack of the Zombie from Planet Kazzoon! Call the police! Call the National Guard!" He hid his head behind his hands.

Gemma threw me the bag then shook a mittened fist at him.

"I'll get you for that, squirt," she said. "You wait. Once we're outside. *Sploosh!* Headfirst into a snowbank." She was trying to sound angry, but you could hear the laughter in her voice.

"That voice!" Michael said. "That's Gemma's voice!"

"Of course it's my voice."

Michael turned to me with a look of absolute terror

12

on his face. "Jon! It's too late! *That thing has eaten Gemma!*"

Even while I was laughing I reached out into the cold, grabbed a small handful of snow off the top of the mailbox next to the door, squeezed it into a sort of mutated snowball, and threw it at him. It missed, all but a few little pieces, but it startled him into shutting up.

While I picked up and wiped up the rest, he said, "Wait till I get *you* outside."

Our house is at the bottom of a hill, and the backyard of Mrs. Andre, across the street, had the best sledding hill in town. Mrs. Andre welcomed kids using her yard; Mom says we're lucky to have that kind of neighbor.

We got into our snow gear as quickly as we could, then headed outside. We tramped across the relatively shallow snow to the garage to get our sleds. Then we more or less waded across the street to ask permission, just in case.

That done, we hit the slope. On the first few trips the snow was too deep and soft for real speed, but after a while we packed it tight and were positively zooming down the hill. It was worth each long trek back up.

At least Michael was big enough to make each climb on his own now. Up to a couple years ago, I used to have to haul him back up the hill on the sled.

The really amazing thing was that we had the whole place to ourselves. I said so to Gemma. "The place is usually crawling with kids by now."

"Sure," she said. "They're waiting until we get the snow nice and fast for them."

Michael, who had just started up the hill, yelled, "Jeep!"

"What?"

13

"Gemma's mother has a Jeep! Most of the other kids can't get here."

As usual, the genius turned out to be right. A few more kids came by, but almost all of them were from our block. With less of a crowd, we got more turns on the hill, and for the first time *I* could ever remember, we felt tired while we were still outside.

Even my brother, who I swear runs on solar energy, was looking worn out. We'd had a good long day, and we knocked off early (for us). We had one last race down the hill, which I won, not because I'm a great sledder or anything, but because I was the heaviest. Then we headed back across the street and home.

It wasn't twilight, but the sun was pretty low in the sky as we headed off to the garage to put the sleds away. At least, I went to the garage. I pulled the door open against the resistance of the snow, stowed my sled inside, and turned around for Michael to hand me his.

Only he wasn't there.

"Michael, come on, I'm freezing out here!" I yelled.

He didn't answer me. Instead, Gemma's voice came. "Jon, come here a minute."

There was something odd in Gemma's voice, a shakiness where I was used to hearing only confidence.

"Be right there," I said, and stomped off to join them.

Gemma was standing at what I would guess to be the edge of the driveway, standing next to Michael, staring.

I joined them to see what they were gaping at.

There was a line of footprints in the snow. They weren't like any footprints that had ever walked across our backyard before. If I had to make a guess, I'd say they were the prints of a miniature baby elephant. Only with toenails.

"What the heck *is* it?" I said.

Without taking her eyes off them, Gemma said, "Got me."

"I know what they are," Michael said. Then he stopped. He can drive you crazy sometimes.

"*Well?*" I said.

"It's a baby stegosaurus," he said.

Gemma rolled her eyes. "Yeah, right," she said.

"Second time I've seen them," my brother went on. "Only this time . . ."

I was nearly frantic. "Spit it out, kid! This time, *what?*"

"This time," he said solemnly, "they're heading for the house."

THREE

"Now, hold on just a cotton-picking minute, here," I said. "Are you trying to tell me there's a baby stegosaurus in the house?"

The genius thought it over. "No," he said at last. "The footprints go to the cellar hatch, but it looks like the padlock is there, undisturbed."

He pointed a mittened hand. I looked and saw he was right. The weird prints went right up to the house itself, to the green metal doors of the cellar. Not only that, but the snow on the doors had been tumbled around and scratched at.

But as Michael had said, the big brass padlock was still in place. It had never been unlocked in all the time we'd been there. I didn't even know if Mom had the key.

"So where's the stegosaurus?" I demanded.

"I'm trying to figure that out," he said.

Gemma started walking away. "Where are you going?" I asked.

"Following the tracks backward," she said. "If we don't know where it is, maybe we can figure out where it came from."

It didn't take her long to check, and she didn't find

anything out. The tracks only ran about twenty yards, from the side of the garage to the cellar hatch. Gemma stood near the garage door with one hand on her chin, thinking. Then she stepped to the door itself and flung it open.

"Aha!" she exclaimed.

"What is it?" Michael asked. His eyes were wide.

"In the garage!" she said. "A big pile of dinosaur poo!"

She cracked up, and so did I. Strangely, Michael didn't. Usually anybody mentioning the word "poo" sent him off into hysterical laughter. As I said, he may be a genius, but he's still a kid.

"Not funny," he said. He went back to staring at the tracks.

It was time to put on my Big Brother hat and get things together around here.

"All right," I said, "fun's fun. But let's get real, okay? There's no dinosaur poo, because there's no dinosaur. We're about a hundred million years too late."

"Sixty-five million," Michael said.

"Oh, excuse me," I said. I admit I was sarcastic. "Still, it's not like we're talking about just missing them, even so."

But Michael was going to be stubborn, something he is very, very good at. He kind of stuck out his lower lip and said, "That's a stegosaurus footprint. I checked in my book after I saw the first one."

" 'The first one.' You keep saying that," Gemma observed. "When was this?"

"About a week ago, when we had that warm spell, and there was mud all over. I saw it out by the creek."

"And you didn't say anything about it?" I had trou-

17

ble believing this. A kid who corners you to tell you about the Slarn of Taros isn't going to be shy about finding a dinosaur in his backyard.

"I didn't think anybody would believe me," Michael said. "Besides, I warned Mom."

"Yeah," I said, "a stegosaurus in the kitchen. You've seen them there, too?"

"No, I just figured Mom would be safe if it stayed outside. I knew from the size of the footprint it had to be a baby one."

The size of the footprint. That made me remember something.

"Wait a minute," I said. "I just thought of something I saw on TV."

"The 'Last Dinosaur' cartoon show," Gemma said.

"No," I said. "This was a show about myths and monsters. There was a part about how people can mistake a wildcat's or bear's paw print for a print made by Bigfoot."

"I saw that show," Gemma said.

Michael shook his head.

"Yes," I said. "Look, the program showed how when the sun hits a footprint in the snow, it grows in all dimensions, and a lot of times changes shape, too. What we've got here is a cat footprint or something that grew by melting in the sun."

Michael kept shaking his head. "The first one I saw was in mud, and it was just this size. Footprints in mud don't melt. If anything, they dry out and shrink."

Gemma was shaking her head, too.

"Oh, great," I said. "Now you're doing it. What's your objection?"

18

"It's a great theory, Jon," she said, "but it's not going to work."

I was really getting steamed. I like to have everything explained in a sensible way. When the two smartest kids I know started trying to sell me an idea I *knew* had to be impossible, that was just too much.

"Why not?" I said.

Gemma pointed at the snow at the tracks down the middle of the driveway.

"We made those tracks. Earlier today when we came and got you guys' sleds, remember?"

"Yeah," I said. "So what?"

"There weren't any prints here then but ours, right? Not even of a bird, let alone a cat."

I didn't want to admit it, so I hedged. "I don't remember any," I said.

She didn't bother to argue. She just said, "Okay. If there were any here, they were too small to notice. Since then, *if* there was anything there, they would have gotten exactly the same amount of sunlight as our footprints, right?"

"Yeah," I said again. "Right, right. What are you trying to prove?"

Gemma put her goggles up on her forehead. When I could see her eyes, I could tell she was as worried as I was.

"Jon," she said quietly, "our footprints are no bigger than they ever were."

I looked. Maybe it's truer to say I gaped.

Now that Gemma had pointed it out, it was obvious that she was right. But I guess Michael isn't the only stubborn one in our family. I went over to one of my tracks and tried to put my foot back in it. Perfect fit. It had been too cold today, and maybe too shadowy here in the driveway, for the sun to have had much effect on our prints.

"Let's go inside," I said. I stowed Michael's sled in the garage, half-expecting to find some dinosaur poop this time. There wasn't any. We went in.

Michael and I went to our rooms to change while Gemma changed in the guest room. Dry and warm now, and out of the wind, the idea of a dinosaur taking a stroll through the snow in our yard seemed silly rather than frightening.

Mom made a breakfast supper. It's sort of a family tradition. Mom and Dad both loved big, hearty, country-style breakfasts, but they were both too tired in the morning to get right up and start frying bacon and eggs and potatoes and mixing and baking biscuits and squeezing oranges and stuff like that.

So every once in a while, especially in the winter time, we'd do all that for supper. I think if Michael and I ever had a meal like that in the morning, we'd be so confused we'd probably go back to bed.

We all dug in. Winter cold and climbing snowy hills takes a lot out of you, and that food was a good way to put it back.

And all through supper, what do you think was all we talked about? Aside from "Please pass the honey," I mean?

Dinosaurs. Or whatever it might have been that made those footprints. Michael said there might have been a time warp, possibly caused by a black hole. It might have whipped a baby stegosaurus into our backyard, then a few seconds later, whipped it right out again.

20

That would explain why the tracks disappeared at the cellar hatch.

What it didn't explain was whether I was supposed to take that seriously or not. I don't really know if Michael understands black holes. It's hard to guess how much of a genius a genius is when you're not one. All I know is I *don't* understand them.

Another thing I didn't understand was Gemma. Outside, she had seemed as unsettled as I was over those darned footprints. Now she was playing silly imagination games with Michael. Her theory was that the footprints had been made by an extraterrestrial who'd been beamed down from his ship near the garage, then beamed back up when he got to the cellar door because his feet were cold.

Even Mom chimed in, asking a few bright questions and smiling at the whole thing. She loves this kind of stuff, says it proves we can be creative.

I skipped being creative that night. I kept my mouth shut, except to shovel home fries into it, and thought.

The only explanation that made any sense was that my best friend and my beloved baby brother had teamed up to pull a gigantic practical joke on me. How they'd done it, I couldn't guess, but as I said before, these are the two smartest kids I know. They could think of a way to fake those prints if anybody could.

Why didn't I say anything? Because until I figured out how they did it, they could just deny the whole thing and give themselves even bigger laughs. If I played dumb and bided my time, I might just get the chance to turn the tables.

Eventually, all the food was gone. Gemma's mom came by and picked her up.

"See you tomorrow at school," she said as she left.

"Unless it snows again," I told her, and we laughed.

After she was gone, Michael helped Mom clear the table while I went upstairs and gathered our clothes to wash. It's hard to believe you can sweat so much when it's so cold out, but you can.

The inside door to the basement is in the kitchen. As I passed by, I told Mom that I was about to do some laundry, so I would leave the dishes in the dishwasher until the load of clothes was done, then I'd start the dishes. Usually, I start the dishwasher up right away. But our water pressure isn't the greatest, so it doesn't make sense to run both appliances at once.

I carried the stuff on down to the basement. Our house is old, built before the idea of a playroom in the basement had ever been thought of. They kept coal in basements like ours (though there's been gas heat there since before we ever moved in), and vegetables that would keep through the winter in a cold place.

Which the basement certainly was. Whoever thought of putting the washer and dryer down there must have done it in the summer. Either that, or he was a polar bear.

I got the stuff in the machine, added detergent, set the controls, and went back upstairs.

Mom was in her favorite chair, again, looking at legal papers, and Michael lay on the floor watching "Jeopardy" and getting most of the questions right. I didn't do too badly myself.

Then, about halfway through "Wheel of Fortune," I could feel the vibrations through the floor that told me the washer had gone into spin cycle. When they stopped, I knew the load had finished.

On the way through the kitchen again, I stopped to get the dishwasher going. It started making that odd sound again. I'd have to look into that.

Downstairs, I went to the machines, switched on the bare lightbulb, got the box of dryer sheets from the shelf, tore one off, put it in the dryer, then started adding clothes.

As I bent over the washer, digging out the clothes, I felt some warm air on the back of my neck, almost like someone breathing on me.

At the same time, I became aware that the basement, usually Gloom City, had gotten really bright.

Oh great, I thought. Lightbulbs do that sometimes before they blow. I looked up. The lightbulb seemed fine.

I turned around. What I saw made me fall back against the washing machine.

Because I wasn't looking at the dust-covered junk we usually kept in our basement. I was looking deep into a yellow-skied, steaming jungle. Forms I couldn't identify were soaring in the distant sky. (Yes, the *sky*. In my own basement.) The plants looked tropical, but that was all I could make out of them.

And standing about seven feet away from me, just where the sensible concrete of our basement floor gave way to wet black jungle dirt, stood a purplish gray creature about the size of a small baby elephant.

I wasn't the dinosaur expert my brother was, but when I saw the plates on its back like upside-down home plates, and the stubby little spikes on its tail, even I could tell it was a baby stegosaurus. I even recognized the footprints in the soft earth around him.

While I looked at that dinosaur, it looked at me.

Its yellow eyes were open wide. It tilted its head and said, *"Neep?"*

"No," I said. This was a dream, or an illusion. I was tired from behing outside all day, that's all. My brain had been filled with dinosaur stuff, and now I was getting a playback. That's all it was.

I rubbed my eyes, but the dinosaur didn't go away.

I walked forward waving my arms.

"Beat it!" I said. "Shoo! I know you're not real, so get out of here!"

I could feel myself walk off the concrete and onto soft dirt. As I advanced, the creature backed up, but not quickly enough. My flailing left hand caught him in the snout.

"Ow!" I said, as he nipped me with his sharp little beak.

I froze just long enough to think that hallucinations do not bite.

Then I ran for my life.

I was moving so fast by the time I hit the living room that I tripped on the edge of the rug and almost crashed headfirst into the TV set.

It was embarrassing, but it did get Mom's undivided attention. "Jonathan," she said, "what *is* the matter?"

I don't know what was going faster, my mouth or my heart. I knew I was babbling, and though I wanted to be calm, I just couldn't stop myself. I guess I got the key words—stegosaurus, basement, and jungle—across, because when I finally ran out of breath, Mom gave me a stern look.

"You shouldn't tease your brother like that, Jon. How did you hurt your hand?"

I was about to protest that I wasn't teasing anybody, that I really had had a run-in with a dinosaur, honest, but Michael caught my eye and gave me a solemn little shake of the head. That, and the look on Mom's face, convinced me to let it go.

Instead, I said, "I, ah, nipped it while I was putting the clothes in the dryer." Even through my shock and frustration, I was pretty proud of that answer. It wasn't completely true, yet it let Mom believe I'd caught it in the dryer door or something.

"Let's see it," Mom said. I gave her my hand. She looked at it and said, "Hmmm. Well, fortunately the skin's only scraped, not broken. Better go put some peroxide and a Band-Aid on it."

"Yes, Mom," I said.

"I'll go with him," Michael volunteered. "It's hard to put on a Band-Aid one-handed."

Ordinarily, I would have told him I could manage just fine. I went along this time because I wanted to get him alone and talk to him.

We keep first-aid stuff in the medicine cabinet in the bathroom off the guest room. I got out the brown hydrogen peroxide bottle, put a little of the liquid on a cotton ball, wiped it across the place at the base of my thumb where I'd been bitten, and watched it bubble up. When Michael was about three years old he asked me what the bubbles were. I told him they were caused by the tiny death screams of millions of bacteria. He really liked that.

"It really was a stegosaurus," I said.

"I know."

"I apologize for doubting you before."

"Forget it. I know it's hard to believe. Tell me about the jungle."

So I guess I babbled about the jungle, too. "I don't know what else to tell you. It was a jungle. It was hot and wet—that's what I noticed first, the hot, wet air— and it seemed to go on forever."

"Did it smell?"

"Come to think of it, it did. Like driving down to Florida last summer."

"Jon, we've got to go back there and check this out."

"Why don't you just shoot me now?" I asked. "It will be less embarrassing than dying of fright."

"It's probably gone by now," Michael said. "You know that."

"I do?"

"Sure," he said. "Otherwise you wouldn't have left Mom downstairs all alone."

I gulped. Actually, I hadn't given it a thought. It's hard for a kid to think of a parent as someone he ought to be protecting.

"Oh, right," I said. "Of course."

Then I had another horrible thought.

"Michael," I said. "What if this baby stegosaurus had some kind of prehistoric mouth germs that modern science doesn't know how to deal with?"

He scratched his chin. You could have put a caption on the picture: GENIUS AT WORK.

"I wouldn't worry about it," he said. "Hydrogen peroxide kills germs by more or less burning them up with pure oxygen. I don't expect prehistoric germs were any more resistant than the modern ones."

The words were comforting, but that didn't stop me from imagining all kinds of disgusting things going on under the bandage. I tried to keep my mind off it.

"Okay," I said. "I suppose we do have to go down there and check, but how? The last load is in the dryer—I wouldn't be picking it up until tomorrow after school under normal circumstances."

"If there is school," Michael reminded me. "It might snow again."

"Whatever. My point is, if I go down to the basement again tonight, Mom is going to get suspicious. If we go down there together, it's really going to look strange."

27

"We'll have to wait until after she goes to sleep, and sneak down."

Just then Mom's voice came from downstairs. "Boys? Is everything all right?"

"Yeah, Mom," I said. "We're fine. We were just coming down."

I don't know why I said that. What I wanted to do was sit down with the genius and work this out, but once the words were out of my mouth, of course we had to do it, or Mom would wonder what was up.

So down we went and pretended to watch that silly tape. All the while I imagined my hand turning a dull green and dropping off, or growing bumpy skin and claws like a reptile's. When the picture was over, Mom said it was bedtime, and I practically leaped to my feet; I was astonished when Michael argued for more time. Then I realized that he was being smart again. It would have been unnatural for us to go to bed without at least a token protest.

We whispered strategy as we went up the stairs. We would set our alarms for two in the morning. Mom hasn't been really great at sleeping at night since Dad died, but even she ought to be out by then. Then we'd meet and go down to the basement.

I set my alarm, but I didn't sleep. I worried. I worried that my hand didn't hurt—no doubt the prehistoric germs were getting started by killing the nerves. I worried what would happen if a full-grown diplodocus, say, should get the idea of squeezing out into the basement. He could uproot the whole house. Of course if that happened, Mom would have to believe me. If we lived through it.

Mostly I worried that I had somehow gone completely

nuts, and Michael was just humoring me. Maybe I *had* pinched my hand in the dryer door and was imagining the rest. I worried about that a lot.

I jumped a mile when the alarm went off. After dressing quickly, I went to the door for a quiet look into the hallway. Then I jumped another mile. Michael was standing right there, his hand poised to knock.

"I checked Mom," he said. "Her light is out."

"Good," I told him. I looked him over. "Go put on some shoes," I told him.

"To go to the basement?"

"In case it's *not* the basement. Believe me, you wouldn't want to go walking barefoot in that jungle."

Michael looked thoughtful. "Be right back." He came back in a few seconds with his sneakers on. It's nice to think of something a genius hasn't.

Of course, if *I* were a genius, I would have thought of putting on the shoes just before we went down the basement stairs. As it was, trying to sneak through the darkened house was excruciating.

We entered the basement and, mercifully, turned on the light.

It was the same old basement: gray-painted walls and a bunch of junk. A woodworking bench that nobody had used since Dad died. Cold and quiet.

Maybe I was nuts. I didn't know whether to be disappointed or relieved.

I said as much to my brother, but he didn't respond. Michael had that stern look of concentration he gets when he's thinking about something real hard.

He looked at the basement as if a whole parade of dinosaurs was passing by. Maybe, I thought, *he's* the one who's nuts.

Michael walked over to the corner, where the washer and dryer were. I followed. Michael pointed at the floor and said, "Look!"

I looked where indicated and saw some brown lumps on the gray floor.

"Dinosaur poo?" I asked.

He gave me his how-can-you-be-so-stupid look. "Jon," he said. He was being patient. "Jon, dinosaur poo would almost certainly be grayish and liquidy, like bird poo."

"Gee," I said, "how silly of me."

"I wish it was dinosaur poo," he said. "If you had some fresh dino droppings, you ought to be able to get someone to believe you have a dinosaur around."

"What is it, then?"

He bent over and picked up one of the lumps and crumbled it in his fingers.

"Dirt," he said. "Jungle dirt. Swamp dirt. Smell."

He put some in my hand, and I felt the moist, springy texture of it. Then, as it warmed, I caught the slightly sickening smell of rotting vegetation coming from it, and I gave an involuntary jerk, as though the stegosaurus was coming back for me.

"It must have come from the dinosaur's foot when he walked up to you," Michael theorized.

"Or my slipper. I took a few steps in there, too."

When I heard what I was saying, I took my little brother by the shoulders. "Michael, this really happened didn't it? I mean, I'm not nuts, right?"

He grinned. "Well, not about this, anyway." When he grins, he looks his age, but the grin never lasts long. In this case, the stern little professor was back in about two seconds. "It's a time warp. Has to be. Maybe a space warp, too, but definitely a time warp. But what's causing it? A black hole?''

That sounded good to me, but before I could say so, he said, ''Nah! A black hole wouldn't cause an intermittent warp; it would be open all the time.'' He started muttering something, probably equations.

''Come on, Michael,'' I told him. ''You'll be more comfortable doing this in your own room.''

He let me lead him away. As I did, I was doing some of my own muttering. I was saying, ''So I'm not nuts,'' over and over again.

And I wasn't nuts. I was just very, very scared.

Marsdentown isn't too big a place, so there's only one school, imaginatively named the Marsdentown School, a low, rambling, brick building on the south side of town, built way back in the 1960s. It's a K through 8 school; Gemma and I have a year and a half left. Then we'll go to the Winnewaug, the big regional high school up in Northbury.

There are two lunch shifts. Seventh graders go in the late shift, and as I was going in, I saw my brother coming out.

"Did you tell her yet?" he asked eagerly.

I shook my head.

"Why not?" he demanded.

Kids. Sometimes they think you can make the world go exactly the way you want it. I hadn't spoken to Gemma yet because I hadn't had a chance.

Oh, I'd *talked* to her—we're in a lot of the same classes—but I hadn't said anything about last night. I hadn't had the chance. The teachers were so happy at getting us back into their clutches, and so eager to make up for time lost to snowstorms, that I barely had time to sneeze, let alone get a chance to tell Gemma my crazy story.

I told Michael I'd take care of it over lunch.

"You better," he said.

I told him to get back to class, not that it would have mattered if he had been late. I sometimes think my genius brother goes to school for social reasons. The second grade is certainly not going to teach him anything he hasn't already read on his own. I doubt the eighth grade could.

Anyway, he went. I spotted Gemma coming in and managed to get behind her in line.

"Sit with me today," I told her.

"I always sit with you," she said as she grabbed a plate of fish fingers and macaroni and cheese, a little plate of limp salad, and a few Jell-O cubes in a paper cup. I went for the ravioli and the cookies. They make you take the salad.

"I mean alone," I told her.

She fluttered her orange eyelashes. "Why Jon, this is so *sudden*."

I probably blushed. Her and her sense of humor. "Ha, ha," I said. "Come on, Gemma, this is important."

"Okay, okay. Can't you stand a little teasing?"

"I didn't get a lot of sleep last night."

We had to walk by our usual table to get to the one way over in the corner where nobody ever sat because it was too near the entrance to the teachers' lunchroom. As we did, the usual gang, Gus and Hector and Iris and Sam and Will, all looked at us and went, "Wooooooo, they want to be *alone*," and this time, I think Gemma blushed. By now, though, that juvenile stuff was the least of my worries.

We sat down. I let Gemma take a few bites, then I told her I apologized.

"What for?"

"For doubting you, yesterday, when you and Michael proved logically that it had to be a dinosaur's footprint we saw."

She grinned. "Oh. Yeah, that was fun, wasn't it?"

Fun wasn't exactly the word that sprang to my mind, but I let it pass. I swallowed hard a couple of times. Then I told her what had happened last night.

"Get real, Jon. Fun's fun, but don't be ridiculous."

"I'm not being ridiculous! Do I seem like I'm trying to pull a joke on you?"

She scratched her freckled chin and looked at me through narrow eyes. "No," she said. "No, you don't. And as a liar, you stink. You could never fake being this sincere without my getting wise to you . . ."

Her voice trailed off.

"But you still don't believe me."

"Well, I mean, a time warp in your basement! It's like something my father would make up."

Now I smiled. Gemma's father was a big, burly, friendly guy with dreamy blue eyes behind thick glasses. He wrote science fiction stories for a living, and was pretty successful. Gemma said weird teenagers were always turning up at their doorstep to meet her father, like he was some kind of mystic wise man or something.

"One of the things Michael and I have thought of was asking your father about this."

Gemma shook her head.

"Bad idea."

"How come?"

"Because Dad would hear what you said and treat it like a story idea. 'Not bad,' he'd tell you, 'only instead of the basement, make it the locker room at Yankee

Stadium in New York. And instead of dinosaurs, make them two-headed silicon creatures from the planet Gzznork.' "

I cracked up.

"You're laughing, but that's *exactly* what Dad would do. He writes this stuff, but he doesn't *believe* any of it."

"I've read some of your father's books," I said. "He would never use a hokey planet name like 'Gzznork.' "

"That's not the point. The point is, he wouldn't be any help." Then her green eyes got bright. "I know!" she said. "That dirt! Dirt is made up of decaying plants and stuff. There are bound to be some molecules in it that don't exist today. That ought to be enough proof at least to get some grown-up scientists to look into the thing."

"That's another thing we thought of," I said. "The trouble is, Michael says to do that kind of test, you need microscopes and equipment we could never get hold of here in town. We don't have the money to hire anybody to make the right tests, and we don't have the evidence to convince some professor at State U., say, to run them."

Gemma nodded soberly. "I can see that. 'Please sir, I'm a twelve-year-old kid, please analyze my dirt and tell me if it came from the time of the dinosaurs.' The only question is whether he would kick us off the campus himself or call for the security guards."

"Exactly."

"You need more proof."

"*We* need more proof," I corrected her.

"We? I didn't get bit by a dinosaur in *my* basement."

She pointed to the Band-Aid on my hand. "How is that, by the way?"

"It's nothing," I said. "Practically healed." It was, too. On that count, at least, I'd worried myself sick over nothing. "But Gemma," I went on, "we want you to be in on this with us."

"I'm flattered, but how come?"

"Michael says you were there when we found the footprint, so you deserve not to miss any of this."

"That's sweet," she said. "What do you think?"

"I think that Michael gets so involved in his brain that he can only see the interesting stuff, and he forgets the scary stuff. I can usually handle him all right, but I don't think I can handle him *plus* a time warp and a bunch of dinosaurs. I—"

I stopped suddenly and shook my head. "Boy, will you listen to me? I hear the words coming out of my mouth, and I can't believe how crazy they sound. That's something I need you for. Sooner or later we're going to have to go to grownups on this thing, and you're better at handling them than any kid I know."

"That's because my parents are weird. Nice, but weird."

"Whatever. But the main reason I want your help is that you're my best friend. Anybody but a best friend would be laughing at me right now."

She put out a hand across the table. It felt nice, but I just shook it firmly a couple of times and let it go. I didn't want anybody getting any wrong ideas.

"Okay," Gemma said. "I'm with you. Fearless dinosaur hunters on the prowl."

"Well, more like on the watch. I think we have to

stake out the basement and wait for the time warp to open up."

"So you want me to spend the weekend at your house?"

"We've already cleared it with Mom, but—"

She held up a hand. "Don't worry about a thing," she said.

And by the end of school, she had it all worked out. Her parents were going to be away that weekend anyway, at a science fiction writers convention, and Gemma was supposed to stay with her mother's Aunt Cookie over in the next state. But Gemma phoned her folks and pointed out that Aunt Cookie hadn't been very well, and it would take extra time for them to drop her off there, and since she was invited to stay in our guest room, anyway . . .

It was worth all the change we had to scrounge for the pay phone. Michael and I waited in the school library for Gemma to finish her music lesson. It was flute today, I think. She has perfect pitch and plays about four instruments. Sometimes it seems like I'm surrounded by geniuses.

While we sat there, Michael wanted to discuss strategy. I tried to concentrate on doing my homework. It was darn sure I wasn't going to do much school stuff this weekend.

We worked it the same way Michael and I had— alarms set for 2 a.m. Saturday morning. This time, we agreed we should dress more warmly, jackets and gloves and stuff. The cellar got cold, and we didn't know how long we were going to be there.

We were halfway down the basement stairs when I

noticed Gemma was carrying the small aluminum case that held her flute.

"Why are you bringing that?" Michael asked. "Going to charm the dinosaurs with music?"

"This," Gemma said, "is our alibi. I got the sudden urge to practice, and decided to go to the basement to do it so I wouldn't wake anybody up, but you two decided to raid the refrigerator and heard my music, so you came down to join me."

Michael and I agreed that it sounded goofy enough to work. Grownups enjoy it when their kids do something harmlessly stupid. It gives them something to talk about.

As it was, during the time the minute hand on my watch crawled around the numbers three and a half times, we might as well have been listening to Gemma play the flute. The basement was cold. The basement was dingy. The clumps of prehistoric dirt we'd left down there (there was one wrapped in a Ziploc bag up in Michael's room) had dried and disintegrated to a light brown dust that looked like anybody's old dust.

We were tired and grew a little testy with each other.

I yawned, rubbed my eyes, and was about to declare the night a washout and suggest we go back and get some sleep when I heard a creak above us.

"Mom's up!" I whispered.

Gemma creased her brow. "At a quarter to six on Saturday morning?"

"Insomnia," I said. "Start playing that thing."

She was already opening the case. She took out the parts of the instrument and started twisting them together. Fortunately, the running of water and the clattering rumble of that darned dishwasher (when *was* I going to take a look at that) told me that Mom was cleaning up after the popcorn we'd made the night before. It's something she always does on a sort of automatic pilot, so I knew Gemma would have all the time she needed.

Then I forgot all about the dishwasher, and Mom, and everything except what was going on in front of me.

The space about ten feet in front of us started to wobble, and everything with it, as though someone were warping a television screen. Then the air just . . . just *burst*. Into fragments. Like a circus clown jumping through a paper hoop.

Only there was no clown. Just warm air, and the smell of rotting vegetation, and a jungly landscape with a sky layered in pink and blue.

Gemma caught her breath. If you looked real hard, you could see what looked like pterodactyls flying around a mountain peak in the distance, straight through the middle of the hole.

"Jon," she said quietly, "I apologize."

I smiled. "That's the very same thing I said to Michael."

Michael was indignant. "Apologize? You mean you didn't *believe* in this? Even though we *both* told you?"

Gemma still kept her eyes on the scene before us. The hot air poured on us like some giant animal's breath, and we all unzipped our jackets.

"Don't worry, squirt," Gemma told him. "I believe it now."

"Let's go," I said. "This thing was only open about ten minutes the last time. Let's get in there, grab some stuff, and get out."

"Just a second," Michael said. He walked around behind the hole in the air. "Heck," he said. "I can see you. Can you see me?"

"I never could see you," Gemma said.

"You know what we can see, Michael. Let's hurry before it disappears."

"Okay, okay," he said coming back around. "I'm still trying to find out how it works. Obviously, it only goes in one direction. On the other side, all I can see is basement. The physics of this thing are incredible."

"Let's go," I said again, but nobody went. We were all a little scared.

Finally, after we wasted a good half-minute looking at each other, Gemma said, "This is ridiculous!" She took my hand, and Michael's, and together, we stepped across into that prehistoric world.

It was like stepping into a steam bath. I'd thought the air that leaked out had been hot, but that was nothing to the temperature there once we'd actually stepped across. It was so hot that you forgot about the smell, which was also remarkable.

In five seconds I began to sweat, and in another ten seconds, during which I managed to shed my jacket, I was positively sloshing.

Gemma and Michael were doing the same.

When we were ready for action, I said, "Let's go. Unusual plants, bugs, if you want to risk a bite, anything that can prove we've been here. *Keep the hole in sight at all times!*"

"Fooey," Michael said. "Let's catch that baby stegosaurus!"

I laughed in spite of myself, and Gemma said that while coming home with a baby dinosaur would certainly do the trick as far as proving our case was concerned, she doubted we could bring it off in ten mintues. Michael had to admit she had a point.

So we went specimen hunting. There was no lack of plants. I just picked one of every different-looking thing I could. I kept one eye on my watch. It had been about

41

five minutes since the hole opened up; we should wrap it up in two more minutes, just to be safe. I was about to call out to the others when I spotted a flash of red in the bushes. It was a beetle, built like a ladybug ten times normal size, but bright red and candy-metallic, like a hot sports car. It was so pretty, it was worth a bite even if it wouldn't prove our case. I reached out and cupped my hand gently around him. He was as gentle as a ladybug, too. The bright color must have been to warn predators that he tasted bad, but I didn't intend to eat him, so I didn't care.

That was enough specimen hunting for me. I turned away from the foliage and called to Michael and Gemma. They rejoined me quickly, each carrying a similar armful.

The hole in the sky was still hanging in the same old place, and looking through it, I was almost homesick for the crummy old basement I could see on the other side.

"All right," I said. "We'll bring this stuff back, show it to Mom, and get her to drive us to State U."

"Sure," Gemma said. "We ought to be able to scare up a couple of the right kind of professor, even on a Saturday."

"Exactly. Ready, Michael?"

"Yeah, I got a great bug."

I was just about to say, "Me, too," when my baby brother gave a yell, dropped everything he had, dove to the ground, and wiggled off into the underbrush like a snake.

"Michael!" I yelled. "What do you think you're doing?" I was, in my mind, already back in Marsdentown. I was worrying what Mom would say about the mess he was making of his clothes.

In less than a minute, he was back, holding a small wiggling something in his hands.

"I got it!" he cried. "I got it!" I'd never heard him happier, not even on a Christmas morning.

"What have you got?" Gemma wanted to know.

"Look, look at the fur. It's a prehistoric mammal."

Carefully, he opened up his hands a little, and there we could see the animal—small, gray-brown, and trembling. It looked something like a mouse, except it didn't have big ears. It was uglier than a mouse, too.

Michael pointed to a little fold of skin on the thing's tummy. "Look, it's a marsupial." He cuddled it as if he loved it. "Just think, creatures like this beat out all the mighty dinosaurs. If this doesn't prove we've been to prehistoric times, nothing will . . ."

Michael's voice kind of dribbled off; he was staring over my shoulder.

Gemma and I spun around to see what he was looking at. We turned just in time to see the basement shimmer and disappear as the whole in the air magically mended itself.

For a few seconds, we stood there like a trio of stuffed dummies. Then we started turning round and round, as though the hole was being cute and playing hide-and-seek games with us.

It sank into Gemma first. "Oh, no," she said. "Oh, no, we're trapped."

I wanted to laugh. She'd said it so mildly, as if she were upset that the cafeteria had run out of chocolate milk.

"Okay," I said. "Okay." I knew that wasn't much help, but I couldn't think of anything else to say.

Michael was clouding up to cry. He cries about one-tenth as much as the normal seven-year-old, but when he lets loose, it's a flood.

The worst of it is, he tries to talk at the same time. This time, he said, "We're—*snf*—we're trapped—*hic hic*—and it's—*sob*—and it's *all my fault!*" Then he dissolved into wracking sobs that shook his body as if some invisible bully were hitting him.

Well, now I really didn't know what to do. Michael was berating himself worse than I could ever do it, even if I'd had the time to realize that it was his fault.

"Okay," I said again. "Don't panic."

And that sent Gemma off. Not crying, screaming. "*Don't panic?* Jon, are you *nuts?* Here we are, trapped at the dawn of time, no weapons, nothing to eat, no way to get out of here, and you're telling me not to panic! What am I supposed to do? Call the stupid Flintstones and ask them if they'll rent us a room? Jon, panic is the only thing that makes *sense!*"

I waited until she stopped for breath.

"Are you done?" I asked.

She took a deep breath, held it, then let it out slowly. When it was all gone, she said, "For now. I guess."

"Okay," I said. I was getting tired of saying that. "Listen. We know the hole, the time warp, whatever it is, comes and goes, right?"

"We ought to," Gemma said bitterly.

"Right. So all we've got to do is wait right here, a couple of days, if necessary, for it to open up again. It'll mean sleeping in shifts, and our parents will be worried while we're gone, but we'll get back okay."

She eyed me with suspicion. "That's swell. But what if it doesn't open up again?"

"No reason to think it won't." That was Michael. "I

first saw a dinosaur footprint a week and a half ago."
His voice was still a little watery, but the worst of the
crying was over. "If it's been going on for that long,
it ought to keep going."

"That's no guarantee," Gemma said.

"No guarantees," I agreed. "Just hope."

Gemma nodded. "I'll settle for that, I guess."

We sat down to wait.

We passed the time trying to decide exactly how stupid we had been. We decided coming here in the first
place had been absolutely necessary. So far, a baby
stegosaurus had gotten loose. What, we asked, would
have happened if it had been an adult? Or a tyrannosaurus or something? The whole town could have been
gobbled up before anybody'd had a chance to do
anything.

"I was stupid for going after Mildred here," Michael
said. He was still holding on to the little creature. He
stroked her head. Mildred the Marsupial hissed and tried
to bite him.

"Watch out she doesn't give you prehistoric rabies,"
Gemma told him. "Besides," she went on, "you caught
her, but we all stood around fussing over the miserable
little thing. All we had to do was step through the hole,
and we could have fussed over her to our heart's content
back in our own time. That was the stupid thing."

"No," I said, "the *real* stupid thing was not running
upstairs and dragging Mom downstairs as soon as the
hole opened up. She was right there in the kitchen."

"What good would that have done?" Michael asked.

"We would have convinced a grownup about what
was going on. Which is what we intended to do in the
first place."

"Maybe. Or Mom might be stranded here, too."

I admitted that he might have a point, although inwardly the thought of having Mom here with us sounded pretty good. It was a silly thought—Mom is no outdoorswoman, and I didn't think dinosaurs worried too much about lawyers. It was a kid reaction, that's all. "I want my *mommy!*" I wondered how old a guy had to get before he stopped feeling that way. It was kind of embarrassing.

Anyway, the conversation petered out, and we just sat there feeling miserable, looking at a spot in the middle of the air and hoping.

We stayed that way for hours—it seemed like days—getting hungrier but not wanting to say anything about it. Then the ground started to shake.

It wasn't much at first, just the kind of vibration you feel when a heavy truck is coming down the road, although I remember thinking it had to be a heck of a truck for it to vibrate this spongy ground.

Then it sorted itself out into a series of huge thuds.

Instinct made me get to my feet. Michael and Gemma did the same.

"What is it?" I asked.

"Feels like an earthquake," Gemma said.

"Footsteps," Michael said. "Look!"

He pointed up over my head. I followed his finger to see something sticking up among the trees of the forest, something that wasn't a tree.

It was a long, snaky, blue-gray neck, topped by a goofy-looking grinning head. Every once in a while, the head would curve down and take a big mouthful of treetop. As it came closer, we could see part of an oil-tanker body among the greenery and hear the crash of trees as it bellied them aside.

The shaking of the ground grew louder. The thing didn't move fast, but it was determined, and it was drawing ever closer to us.

Gemma pushed some red hair from her face, maybe to get a better look at it. "Um, guys?" she aid. "This is an impressive spectacle, and all that, but it seems to be heading right for us. What do we do?"

I had been wondering about that same question. On the one hand, if we lost this spot, we might be stranded here forever. On the other hand, if I was going to die in the prehistoric past, I could think of better ways to wind up than as some gunk squished between a dinosaur's toes.

"Let's stand our ground as long as we can," I said. "It might miss us."

My brother said, "Jon, I don't think so. In fact, I think that—"

I never did find out what he thought, because at that second he stopped speaking in order to dodge a falling tree. The dinosaur didn't make a trumpeting sound the way they do in the movies—instead it sort of grunted and wheezed like a very big pig. Somehow, that made it even scarier. It stopped walking for a second to grab another treetop—it treated trees like broccoli spears.

"I think we'd better run," I said.

I didn't have to say it twice. We took off. In the next second, a huge foot crushed down through the space we'd been occupying onto the soft earth below.

Thorns ripped at us, branches slashed our faces, and the rumble of the dinosaur's footsteps was worse than thunder. The real miracle was that we managed to stay together.

Somehow we did. I don't think any of us tried to do it, I just think subconsciously we knew that as bad as being stranded here was, being stranded here *alone* would be a million times worse.

We ran until we collapsed. We didn't go very far for all the energy we put out, fighting through the thick tangle of underbrush, but it was far enough. We'd gotten out of the path of that tree-eating juggernaut—its footsteps were receding in the distance. We found a little clearing—not the one we'd first shown up in—and sat there catching our breath.

After a few seconds, Gemma came over to me, took a tissue out of her pocket, and wiped my face with it. There was blood on it when she took it away.

"Ran through a pricker brush," I said.

"I know, I saw you. Are you all right?"

"Stings a little. I'll be okay."

"None of the scratches seems very deep. How are you, Michael?"

"Out . . . of . . . breath . . . ," he gasped. "But okay."

Gemma ruffled his hair. "Don't worry," she said with a grin, "the squirt's indestructible."

"Gemma," I said.

"Yes, Jon?"

"Remember you panicked a little while ago?"

"Of course I do."

"Well, I hate to tell you this since you seem not to have noticed it, but we are in unbelievably worse shape now than we were a few minutes ago."

"I know that."

"So how come you're not panicking now?"

She shrugged it off. "I got it out of my system. I mean, I'm scared and everything, but screaming won't help it. Screaming never helps, just sometimes you've got to do it." She narrowed her eyes at me. "Why? Are you panicking?"

"Any second now," I told her.

It was true. I could feel my brain racing with the thousand aspects of our problem, and my heart trying to keep up with it.

"Well, if you must," she said, "you must. Anything I can do?"

Her calmness was driving me nuts. It was almost as if when she and Michael were losing it, I *had* to keep under control. Now that they were calm, there was room for me to go to pieces.

"Where's Mildred?" Gemma asked my brother.

"I dropped her when we started to run," Michael said. "I figured she'd have a better chance on her own."

"I hope you got her full name and address—she's our next of kin."

I wanted to laugh at that—having a hissing, snapping,

ugly little marsupial as your next of kin—then I realized that Gemma was right. Here in the dim prehistoric past, nothing on earth was as closely related to the three of us as Mildred and her kind. I'd lost my sports car bug, too.

My panic went away, replaced by a kind of cold gloom. We didn't belong here. This wasn't our world, and wouldn't be for millions of years. We were as alien here as invaders from another planet.

I didn't say any of that. If I had, I would have started blubbering, and that would have a bad effect on Michael's morale. He has an exaggerated idea of his big brother's capabilities, and this wasn't the time to prove him wrong.

So I controlled my voice as well as I could and consulted the genius.

"Michael, where are we?"

He stood up and looked around. "Well, the mountain is closer, but off to the left of where we were before. The sun's going down right behind it—that makes it the west. Some things don't change even over billions of years. The distance is a guess. I'd say we're about a half-mile northwest of where we came through the hole."

"No," I said, "where *are* we? And when? We went through a time warp—we could be anywhere in the universe."

Michael got that concentrated look and shook his head. "Would another planet have evolved creatures *exactly* like a stegosaurus and a diplodocus?"

"That was a diplodocus?" Gemma asked.

"Of course," Michael said impatiently. "Didn't you see the nostril configuration?"

Gemma said, "No, silly me. I missed it."

A lot of people, geniuses or otherwise, might have been smug just then, but Michael never is. It's one of the best things about him. "Yeah," he said, "it was a diplodocus all right. The odds against some other planet evolving two complicated organisms that look *exactly* like earth creatures is so big I can't even guess at it."

Michael stood up and started wiping his hands on his pants. "So," he went on "we're on Earth. Probably still in Marsdentown. Sometime during the Late Jurassic period."

"Oh, joy," Gemma said. "Tyrannosaurus rex. Velociraptors."

There was a fierce frown on Michael's face. "You're thinking of *Jurassic Park,*" he said.

Gemma admitted it.

Michael conceded grudgingly that it was a good movie. "But the title was *wrong*. Practically all the dinosaurs in it were from the Cretaceous period, millions of years after the Jurassic."

I wanted to tell him to relax, that the guy who made the movie wouldn't even be born for another sixty-five million years or so. Then it occurred to me that neither would we, and that was so confusing my brain dropped the subject like a hot brick.

"Michael," I said. I could hear the desperation in my voice. "Somehow we've got to get back to where we were before."

He scratched his chin, leaving some clean streaks in the dirt. "That shouldn't be too big a problem."

This was news to me. "It shouldn't?"

"It's going to take some walking."

"I don't care if it takes swinging from tree to tree with my tongue. How do we do this?"

"Look at the mountain," he said.

"Yeah?" I could still see reptiles flying around its peak.

"See how we're kind of off to the side of it? All we've got to do is head to our left until the mountain looks exactly the way it did when we first got here, then walk straight away from it until we come to some fresh diplodocus tracks."

"Our jackets and gloves and stuff will be there, too," Gemma added.

Now that Michael had explained it, it was simple. I was sure that if I'd come through that hole alone, I'd be dead already. Now that we had a plan, my brain consented to go back to work.

"I think that while we go left, we should go *toward* the mountain at the same time."

"Why?" Michael asked. "That'll just make for a longer walk."

"So we'll be absolutely sure to be in front of the whole when it opens up. Because if we're behind it, we'll never see it even if we're within a couple of feet of the thing."

"It's probably not necessary," Michael said, "but you're right. It's better to be safe."

We started off on a diagonal toward the mountain. Michael led the way; I brought up the rear.

After a few hundred yards, Michael stopped.

"What's wrong?" Gemma asked.

"Nothing. I just had a thought."

"What?" I said.

"I think we ought to break off a few of these branches and carry them along with us."

"I could use a walking stick," Gemma said. "Soft dirt or no soft dirt, my feet hurt."

"Walking sticks, Michael? Is that what you have in mind?"

"Well, yeah," he replied. "That and the fact that there are a lot of kinds of dinosaurs we might run into."

I knew what he meant. Now that the noise of the diplodocus wasn't drowning out everything around, I could hear all sorts of chatterings and slitherings as unseen creatures made their way through the brush. Judging by the sun, I guessed it would be dark in two hours or so; the creatures might be bolder in the dark. I went to a tree and put my whole weight behind pulling off a couple of branches.

As she took hers, Gemma, practical as always, said, "I'll use mine as a walking stick. What good is this going to be against a tyrannosaurus? Might as well hit it on the nose with a rolled-up newspaper."

"You don't have to worry about a tyrannosaurus," Michael told her.

"Why not?"

"Tyrannosaurus is a Late Cretaceous period dinosaur. They won't be around for millions of years yet."

That was some comfort. Gemma was even whistling as we set off.

We hadn't gone far, though, when she whirled around and stared off into the jungle.

"What's the matter?" I asked.

"*Ssssh!*" she said fiercely.

Michael and I rushed to her side, sticks at the ready. They weren't much, but they were all we had.

"What is it?" I said, whispering, this time.

"I thought I saw something."

"What?"

"Forget it, you'll think I'm crazy."

"That's a heck of a way to think about the one who told you he'd been nipped by a stegosaurus."

Gemma didn't like it, but she had to admit I had justice on my side.

"Oh, all right, but it's silly. I . . . well, I thought I saw one of the ferns move."

"Of course you did," I said.

"I mean it, Jon."

"So do I. The ferns are moving all the time, haven't you noticed? Sometimes there's a little breeze, not that it does much good with this heat. Then, there's always critters moving in there, and that shakes—"

"That's not what I'm talking about."

"Oh."

"I thought I saw one of the trees *move*. As in change its position compared to the other ferns."

Michael scratched his head. "Like it was *walking* or something, you mean?"

"Yeah. I said it was silly."

"Well, don't feel bad about it," Michael said. "I've seen something like it, too."

Gemma eyed him suspiciously. "Don't humor me, squirt."

"I'm not. Either you're as tired as I am . . ."

"That sounds pretty likely," Gemma said.

". . . or there's something strange going on here."

I started to laugh, maybe a little hysterically. I was tired, too, after all. "Baby brother," I said, "we're trapped in the past dodging dinosaurs. Isn't that strange enough for you?''

Michael was impatient. "You know what I mean. I just wish we could gather some data and figure out what's going on.''

I shook my head. "This time I get *my* wish, and I wish we get back to where that hole was before dark.''

Gemma voted with me, and even Michael didn't put up too much of a fight. We headed off.

And three minutes later I was running for my life again.

EIGHT

None of us ever did find out what it was the meat eater was chasing—it was moving too fast when it went by me. It moved on four legs, and was sort of a grayish green. Artists these days have been giving dinosaurs all kinds of nifty colors, but all the ones we saw were kind of dull. That was all right—they didn't need bright coloring to get our attention.

Anyway, this grayish-green animal nearly knocked me down, but I still didn't get a good look at it, except for the color, the fact that it went on four legs (and pretty quickly, too), and was about the size of a yearling calf at Gus Franklin's folks' dairy farm south of Marsdentown. Bleated like one, too.

I might have turned and gotten a better look at the prey-to-be, but I was distracted by the sight of what was chasing it.

It strode, on two big clawed feet, and it had little clawed arms just below its head. This one was a sort of grayish yellow, and he had little black eyes on either side of a mouth that looked like a car trunk lined with daggers. Bent way forward the way it was, the mouth was exactly level with my head. Standing up straight, the thing must have been twelve feet tall.

"Gemma!" I yelled, *"Michael! RUN!"* then I tried to follow my own advice. I wanted to cut sideways to avoid it, the way we had with the diplodocus, but I had to be far enough in front of it for that to do me any good. The soft ground seemed to clutch at my sneakers and slow me down, as if invisible hands were trying to serve me up as a snack for the thing behind me.

Then I made a big mistake—I turned around to see if it was gaining on me. Of course, as soon as I took my eyes off where I was going, I tripped on a root or a vine or something and went down, plowing a furrow in the soft dirt.

I tried to get up, but the dirt kept squirting out from under. I rolled over on my back to try to squirm away.

I found myself looking right up into that deadly mouth.

Its breath stank of rotten meat, and a hot drop of dinosaur drool splashed my forehead. I was a speck of dust, and this lizard was the vacuum cleaner that was going to make me disappear forever. I wanted to close my eyes, but I was too scared even to do that, and the dinosaur stepped right over me and went on with the chase.

I lay there, half-buried in soft dirt, not able to believe I wasn't at that very second sliding in chunks into a reptile's gullet. When it finally sank into my brain that I was alive, and more important, likely to stay that way, I started to shiver really hard, as if I were standing hip-deep in snow in bathing trunks, as if I were trying to shake off my arms and legs.

Michael and Gemma ran to me and pulled me into a sitting position and held me together. Eventually, the shakes went away, but I was still breathing hard.

"We thought you were *dead!*" Michael said.

"I knew I was," I breathed. "Why didn't he eat me?"

"Too tough," Gemma said. Then she gave me a little kiss on the cheek. I looked at her, but she just smiled. If the guys in the cafeteria had seen that, it would have taken weeks for me to live it down.

Michael, as always, was giving the question serious consideration. "Maybe you just don't smell like a food," he said. "It's never smelled or tasted a human before."

That seemed like a good bet.

Suddenly, Gemma turned angrily on Michael. "Hey, you little twerp, you said there wouldn't be any tyrannosauruses for millions of years yet!"

"There won't!" the genius protested. "That was an allosaurus, an ancestor of tyrannosaurus. A T-rex would have been much bigger."

I struggled to my feet before the thought of a monster that size bearing down on me could give me the shakes again.

"Maybe he just had a one-track mind," I said. "He decided he was going to have that green thing for dinner, and he didn't want to be distracted by something pale and pink."

Michael nodded. "That makes sense. Good idea, Jon."

"Thank you. Anyhow, he was plenty big enough for me."

I thought carefully about how I worded my next question. Michael has a tendency to take things literally.

"Michael," I said, "is this the worst thing we're going to find?"

"What do you mean?"

"I mean, are we likely to run into anything bigger, meaner, hungrier, or more dangerous?"

"Well, we could run into another allosaurus. Or the same one again."

"I know," I said. I was being patient. "Anything more dangerous than that?"

"More dangerous? No. Allosaurus was the most dangerous thing in Late Jurassic North America."

But as we were soon to find out, he was wrong.

Despite all the distractions, we got positioned on the right side of the mountain again before the sun disappeared behind it. With a decent break, we could be back where we wanted to be by nightfall. How we'd protect ourselves in the dark, and what, if anything, we would eat were things we could worry about when we got there.

Right now, what we wanted to do was to climb a small hill about twenty yards away. It was the only elevated land anywhere this side of the mountain, and it was our only chance to maybe see above the treetops and plot a course back to the site of the time warp.

By this time, though, we were so tired that the little hill might as well have been Mount Everest. Well, not really. We got up it, but we leaned on our sticks the whole way, and we were puffing when we got up there.

Michael, who seems to draw energy from sunlight, like a plant, got to the top first. He stood there gazing down with a stupid look on his face.

"Hey," I said, "you're facing the wrong direction." I was too busy pulling Gemma up to see what he was looking at, so the two of us saw it at the same time.

"Oh, golly," Gemma said, but in this case even her

mother would have forgiven her if she'd cursed and sworn.

There was a *building* down there. And I don't mean a cave or a grass shack. I mean a *building*. Metal and concrete, or something that looked like concrete, anyway. The thing was about the size of one of those small factories or warehouses they have out on Route 8 north of town, except it curved and bumped in odd places. For instance, there were a bunch of silvery bubbles along the walls about two-thirds of the way up, where you'd expect to find windows.

A bunch of spikey things grew out of the roof, each one bent at a different angle and ending in a sort of knob or ornament. It looked like some kind of fantastic metal garden.

The biggest thing up there was something that looked exactly like somebody's backyard TV satellite dish, with the circle of metal mesh surrounding a probe pointing from it.

It made me extremely nervous that the probe part was pointed right at us. I kept expecting a heat ray or something to flash out and fry us, but I couldn't find my voice to say anything about it. Instead, I grabbed Michael and Gemma by the back of the collars and dragged them down with me to lie flat on the top of the hilltop.

"What did you do that for?" my brother demanded indignantly.

A stupid instinct made me whisper my reply.

"I don't think dinosaurs built that, do you?"

Gemma burst in, whispering, too. "Don't be stupid Jon. They don't have any hands, let alone tools. That's an advanced construction job."

"Yeah," I said. "Even I could tell that. It just occurred to me that whoever built that might not be as friendly as they are smart, and maybe we shouldn't make ourselves so obvious."

They agreed that this was good thinking.

After a while, Gemma, still whispering, said, "I just don't get it. Are we in the past or what?"

"I don't know," Michael said, "but I'll tell you one thing. I bet that's what's been causing the time warp. Or whatever kind of warp it is."

"Well, yeah," I said. "Who else is there? *We* certainly didn't do it."

"Look at that place. I bet those silver-bubbles on the side are an array for catching solar energy. And those things on the roof are antennae to broadcast energy at different vibrations."

I knew he was a genius, but enough is enough. "How can you possibly know this?" I demanded.

"I don't know it; I'm just guessing."

Gemma pointed to a big metal rectangle at ground level two-thirds of the way along the side facing us. "What do you guess that is?"

"That?" Michael said, as though it should have been obvious. "I guess that's a door."

And before the words were even out of his mouth, his guess was confirmed, because the large metal rectangle began sliding open.

My mind formed the words *let's get out of here,* but my mouth never said them. Like my brother and my friend, I was going to stay glued to the spot until I saw what came out of that door.

Inside, I was praying like mad it would be a human, somebody on a top-secret experiment or something,

61

someone who could scold us, tell us to keep our mouths shut, and send us home.

It wasn't a human. It was far from human. A dinosaur would have been more comforting.

What came out of the doorway was something that looked like a cross between an octopus and a palm tree. It was about eight feet tall, covered in some brownish, textured stuff that looked like the fake leather you see on cheap furniture. At the top, it split into four evenly spaced thick tentacles that drooped down (when they weren't moving like giant snakes) to about two feet above the ground. Between each pair of tentacles was a round thing, shiny green, like unripe grapefruit. Looking down on it, as we were, we could see that the tentacles surrounded a diamond-shaped spot in the top of the head that opened and closed at about five-second intervals. I figured that was for breathing.

At the bottom, it split into four again, only this time into short, stumpy, rootlike feet on which it could, when it walked, lift itself ten or twelve inches off the ground.

It didn't look as if it liked to walk. It sort of tip-stumped through the doorway with just the feet, moving two at a time. Once it was clear of the building, it whipped two of the tentacles forward at the same time it moved its feet, and it went a little faster. It still wasn't very fast—seemed to me as if the thing used up a lot of energy for a pretty small result.

One thing about it, though. To change direction, it didn't have to turn around, it just changed the combination of feet and tentacles that it used. This let it twist and lurch wherever it wanted to.

If Michael could guess, so could I—those green shiny things were eyes.

It was fascinating to watch. Horrible, but fascinating. The thing twisted its way up and down the building, as if examining it for termites or something. Every once in a while, its body would arch back, as though it wanted to see the roof.

"Inspecting the equipment," Michael whispered.

All the while the creature was doing this, its tentacles hung down and twitched more or less aimlessly. Then, suddenly, it stopped looking at the building and twisted violently until it was lined right up with us—until the point where if my eyes were lasers, they could have burned a hole right through the middle of its trunk. It didn't make me feel happy; if I could tell what its "eyes" were looking at, I might have felt better.

Or worse.

Because now, it raised its tentacles and began making a series of deliberate waves and shapes with them. It also arched itself again so that even I could tell it was looking straight up the hill at us.

"Let's get out of here!" I hissed. This time, I got the words out, and I put them into action, too. All of us did, scrambling to our feet and beginning to run down the hill.

I said *beginning* to run down the hill. We didn't get far. The top of the little mound was now ringed with the creatures, more or less identical. They differed only in shades of brown and green. When we tried to run, they cut off our escape. As we tried to fight, we were wrapped up in strong, rubbery tentacles and dragged down the hill to the building below.

NINE

"So we really *did* see ferns moving," Michael said. He was sitting on the floor of the tall, narrow room the Twisters had thrown us into, leaning against the fine metal mesh that covered the wall. The floors were some sort of plastic, hard but still springy. If humans had the stuff, it would make fine flooring for a basketball court.

Gemma gave a short, bitter laugh. "Only they weren't ferns. They were aliens, tracking us the whole time. As clumsily as they move, why didn't we catch more than a glimpse of them?"

I don't know if she was doing this to keep Michael's spirits up, but it was working. Give him a chance to lecture, and he's happy. "Camouflage. They look like plants, especially plants in a jungle. I've never been in a real jungle—I mean a jungle from our own time, let alone a prehistoric one. We didn't know what didn't belong."

I had a thought, too. "Everywhere we went, I heard crashing in the brush. I just thought the noise was made by creatures running away. But it probably was the Twisters, following us."

"It might have been things running away from *them,* too," Gemma said. "They're scary." She shivered.

"Strong, too," I told her. "I struggled until I almost dislocated my shoulders. I didn't gain an inch. Not only that, but mine held me absolutely captive and didn't even give me a bruise."

"Same here," Michael said, "and they taste terrible."

Together, Gemma and I said, *"Taste?"*

"I bit mine. Not that it did any good. I couldn't even break that skin or hide or whatever it is."

There was silence for a few moments. The light in the room was a dim blue. It made us look to be in even worse shape than we were. I closed my eyes for a second and almost dozed before I remembered how scared I was. And how hungry.

"I wonder what they're going to do with us," Michael announced.

So did I, but I didn't want to talk about it. As a diversion, I said, *"I* wonder what they're doing here in the first place."

"They're trying to conquer the Earth," Gemma said. "Isn't that what aliens always do?"

"How do you know they're aliens?" I countered. "Maybe they're some sort of prehistoric intelligent life that evolved on Earth and vanished, somehow."

"No, Jon," Michael said. "Look at this place. You can't have science to this level without a large-scale civilization behind it."

"So? How do you know they don't have one? This could be an exploring expedition to the unexplored jungle regions of whatever it is they call Earth."

Michael shook his head. "That's not my point. If they had a civilization at this level on Earth at the time of the dinosaurs, even atomic war wouldn't have wiped it out so bad that we wouldn't have found fossils of it by our time.''

That made sense. Unfortunately, it cut off the argument I was trying to get going to keep ourselves (me in particular) distracted from the gibbering hysterics that would follow if we let ourselves concentrate on the fix we were in. I figured it was just about the worst fix any three humans had ever faced.

Something else, something else to talk about, to keep our minds occupied.

"Okay, Gemma, you say they're out to conquer the Earth. Haven't they already done it?"

Gemma didn't want to play. "What are you talking about, Jon?"

"This is the Jurassic period. Until we showed up, they were the only intelligent life Earth had ever seen. Boom. Instant conquest.''

"There's still the dinosaurs." She said.

"They've got some way to handle the dinosaurs," I told her. "Otherwise, they'd have been stomped before they got the land around here cleared and the building put up.''

Michael mumbled something. I asked him what he said.

He mumbled again.

"Speak up.''

This time he practically shouted it. "Time warp!''

"What about it?" Gemma said.

"They came from somewhere, landed here, and set up the time warp.''

"In our basement," I reminded him.

"Yeah," Michael mused, "that is kind of puzzling. You'd think they'd set it up into the basement of the

White House or something, then send an allosaurus to eat the president.''

"Maybe you can suggest it to them," Gemma said.

Suddenly Michael was very seven years old. "You take that back!"

"Hey, squirt, it was just a joke."

"It's not funny. I wouldn't help them. What kind of rat do you think I am?"

"All right, all right," she said. "Take it easy. You're not a rat. I know you wouldn't help them any more than I would."

"That's better. What was I talking about?"

"The time warp," I said.

"Oh, yeah. They wouldn't be messing around with the time warp if they were happy conquering dinosaurs; they'd just go ahead and build their civilization."

Michael's words were beginning to make a horrible kind of sense. I had the feeling my attempts at distraction were going to turn out to be a dismal failure.

"You mean . . ." I said.

"Uh-huh," Michael said. "For some reason, they're not happy with conquering dinosaurs. They want to conquer the late twentieth-century human race. They want to conquer *us*."

Oh, boy, I thought, if the three of us represented the late twentieth-century human race, the Twisters were off to a good start. I don't know about the other two, but I was trapped in a well of gloom so deep I didn't think I'd ever get out.

It wasn't that I didn't know what to do. I knew what to do as well as if Ms. Betts had written it on the blackboard for a homework assignment. You could say it in a sentence. I had to get out of there, stop or delay the Twisters, get Gemma, Michael, and me back safely to our own time, warn the authorities, and make them believe it.

Only trouble was, at the moment, I couldn't even figure out a way to wash my face, get a drink of water, or find something to eat.

Then the door opened, and the last of those problems was solved. A Twister lurched in, using only his stumps. He didn't have enough room to swing his tentacles, and he couldn't, anyway, since they were carrying things— a bucket of water, and a plastic thing like a basket that contained a bunch of colorful shapes. I took these to be fruit, although among the stuff were a couple of round green things that looked exactly like the Twisters' eye-balls, if that's what they were.

The Twister put the things down in the middle of the room and started making signals with his tentacles, like a Boy Scout doing semaphore, only more complicated and without the flags. It was obvious that this was how they spoke to each other.

"Yeah," Gemma said. "Same to you, thanks. Sorry, no tip. I left my change umpty millions years from now."

The Twister stopped and looked at her. Well, since it had eyes all around, it was always looking at every-thing, but at least it bent in Gemma's direction. It reached into the basket, grabbed an orange thing that was probably the distant ancestor of the mango, and stuffed it down the hole in the top of his trunk between the tentacles.

"Right," Gemma said. "We're supposed to eat it. We probably will—what can it do, kill us? But we have an Earth taboo about eating in front of monsters, okay? So would you please scram?"

The Twister made a short hissing sound out of its tophole. Then from a fold in the skin on its trunk it took a small plastic gadget. It wrapped the thing in the very end of its tentacle, down where the tentacle was thin as a finger and flexible as a monkey's tail, and squeezed it.

Michael said, "Hey!"

Tired and warn out as I was, I jumped up and made a dive for him, but I got swatted away by a spare tentacle.

Gemma put her hands up in front of her face and tried to back away right through the wall.

The object in the Twister's tentacle let out a sound, similar to one of the "boops" you hear when you push a button on a touch-tone phone, but more complicated and a little louder.

I waited for a flash of light, a scream from Gemma, some kind of indication that the weapon was working.

What happened was that the door slid open. The creature lurched out of the door. I was too far away to make it through the opening, and I don't really know if I would have had the guts to try. In a few seconds, the booping sound came again, and the door closed.

Michael did something totally out of character. Two things. First, he didn't say anything. Second, he rushed to Gemma and put his arms around her.

Gemma sat there, patting him absentmindedly on the back, with a look on her face as if she were staring at something a thousand miles away.

"I know how you feel," I said.

She shook her head as if to clear it, then said, "Huh?"

"I felt the same way when the allosaurus ran over me."

"What? Oh, no, it isn't that. I mean I was scared all right, but just now, I was thinking of something."

"Like what?"

"Forget it, just a silly notion. Let's eat."

We ate. After all, what could it do to us that was worse than what we were already facing? The fruit turned out to be good, sweet and juicy, with that pineappley taste that all tropical fruit seems to have. We drank water from the bucket, then used some to wipe our faces off.

It's a strange thing. Being full and a little cleaner made an enormous difference. As far as I knew, we weren't the teeniest bit closer to saving our civilization (or even ourselves), but I felt less hopeless about it. I felt that somehow, we'd at least make a try at it.

After we'd about emptied the basket, Michael said, "Jon?"

He sounded tentative. Very unlike him.

"What is it, Michael?"

"I want to go to sleep."

"Might as well. They didn't give us a TV set."

Gemma snickered, but Michael stayed serious. "Can I sleep next to you?"

"Sure," I said. I waved him over to me. He sat next to me against the wall, put his head on my chest, and in about a minute and a half he was making little-boy snores in his nose.

A little while after that, Gemma came over and sat on the other side of him. "So he doesn't fall over in his sleep," she said.

"Gem," I said. "I'm sorry."

"For what?"

"For getting you into this."

She looked at her arm. "I don't see any twist marks, do you? I'm flattered you asked me."

That made me feel better. After a minute or two, she said, "Jon? Whatever happens, don't give up hope, okay?"

"Okay," I said. A few minutes after that, we were all asleep.

I woke up with a scream. A rubbery tentacle, wrapped around my upper arm, was shaking me. I opened my eyes and found myself looking right into one of the green globes of a Twister, I think the same one that brought us the food.

He pulled me to my feet, not too roughly, then let me go. Of course, my scream had awakened Gemma and Michael, and they got up, maybe a little confused, but angry and ready to fight.

"It's all right," I told them. "I think he just wants us to come with him."

Not having any heads, naturally, the Twisters couldn't nod, but I thought I saw one of the tentacles hooking toward the door in a gesture I could recognize.

It seemed to work. We headed toward the tall, thin door, and behind us, the Twister used the booper thing and opened it. As we went through, Gemma was humming. I remember thinking that not giving up hope was fine, but this was completely silly.

He led us into the main room, a place we'd barely glimpsed before, since we were struggling against tentacles when we'd come through it the last time.

It was big enough to play a decent game of volleyball in, or it would have been if there hadn't been so much stuff in it. The stuff was mostly electrical equipment:

weird, asymmetrical stuff with rods and disks sticking off them at odd angles. Also, the Twisters didn't believe in hiding wires. Everything seemed to be wrapped in multicolored spaghetti.

The ceiling here was even higher than the one in our . . . well, I guess our "cell" would be the best word for it. That made sense, since if a Twister lifted a tentacle straight up, it could be almost fifteen feet tall. Again, the light came from the ceiling without any visible source. It was still bluish, but brighter than it had been, nearly bright enough to hurt our eyes, especially after just having woken up.

"The light is blue because their planet circles a hotter star than ours does, right?" I asked my brother.

"Very good, Jon," he said. He sounded like a college professor or something, congratulating a slow student who's finally caught on to a different concept. I don't mind, really, except that the last time I'd been talking to him, he was just a cute little guy, and I was his big brother, protecting him from harm so he could sleep. Sometimes the changes are hard to keep up with.

The Twister shepherded us to a clear spot on the floor, part of a pathway through the equipment that ran from the door to the outside to the door of the cell.

He raised the two tentacles closest to us in a "stop" gesture, then walked behind a C-shaped desk about four and a half feet tall. The surface of the desk was broken up into a bunch of narrow levers, like piano keys, only all black. The Twister brought his tentacles down to the semicircular keyboard all at once, and moved them faster than human eyes could follow.

A voice like thunder seemed to shake the building. *"WHAT ARE YOU DOING HERE?"*

The volume made us wince.

The Twister reached out above the keyboard, flipped a few switches, and tried again.

"What are you doing here?"

That was better. The sound was raspy and insistent, but at least it wasn't going to pop our eardrums. I looked around for a loudspeaker, but I couldn't find one. Like the blue light, the sound seemed to be coming from everywhere.

"What are you doing here?" it repeated.

"Heck with that!" Michael piped up. "What are *you* doing here?"

It's incredibly frustrating to deal with a creature with no face to speak of and only a mechanical voice. Now it said, "There is no time for that."

The trouble was, what did it mean? If a human said those words, even over the phone where you couldn't see him, you could tell if he was angry or impatient or even amused by Michael's question. Here, we got no clues.

The Twister tried the keyboard again. "How did you come to be here? How did you activate the chronic discontinuity?"

"The what?" Gemma asked.

"Time warp," Michael supplied.

"Oh," she said. Then she turned to the Twister. "How did *we* activate it? Are you crazy or what? You're the ones who were turning dinosaurs loose in the snow. We were only trying to figure out what was going on."

"You did nothing to activate the chronic discontinuity. That is your statement?"

"That's right," I said.

"That cannot be true. The equipment has been calibrated and recalibrated. You have been adding a frequency that misplaces and prematurely activates the chronic discontinuity. You must explain."

"Go suck a pickle," I said. "We don't know anything, and we're not going to tell you anything."

Michael grabbed my hand. Gemma said, "Way to go."

The Twister hit a few more switches, then hit the keyboard.

It was like a knife through my head.

Before my eyes squeezed shut in agony, I could see that Michael and Gemma were feeling it, too. I clapped my hands over my ears, but it did no good.

I doubled over with the pain, but I exerted all my strength and kept myself on my feet. I didn't want to give the stinking monster the satisfaction of seeing me roll around on the floor. It was stupid, but somehow important.

He let go of the keys, and the pain went away. All gone, all at once. My ears weren't even ringing.

"We dislike causing pain," the voice said. "Please do not make it necessary."

"Go ahead and tell him, Jon," Gemma said.

"Yeah," Michael added. "It can't do them any good."

"All right," I said. "I'll tell you. But then I want to ask *you* some questions."

I don't know who I thought I was kidding. I was a prisoner, and with that earbuster gimmick, the Twister could probably wind up having me fetch sticks for him. Somehow, I didn't think he'd have a whole lot of trouble getting over his dislike of causing pain.

"Proceed."

"Okay, then—What do I call you?"

"There is no sound for the symbol of my identity. We use vibration as a tool; we are not equipped for vocal communication. To the others of my kind I am—" He took his tentacles from the keys and did a little stylized dance with them. "Proceed," the voice came again. "I have made a special study of your type and designed this machine to communicate. I had not thought to use it so soon. I will hear and understand. There is no need to use a sound for the symbol of my identity."

Wonderful, I thought. No face, no voice, no name. This was a tough guy to relate to.

"Call him Slarn," Michael suggested.

I laughed in spite of myself. Slarn was the name my brother gave to at least seventy percent of his fantasy aliens.

Well, I thought, why not?

"Is it okay if I call you Slarn?"

"If it will hasten your imparting of the information we require."

"Okay, Slarn, here goes."

So I told him. The whole story, up till the time they

caught us. As Michael said, it couldn't do them any good. They'd have to get the information they required some other way.

"Your story seems truthful."

I was glad to hear that. If a monster from outer space had called me a liar, I would have been very upset.

The mechanical voice went on. "It is, however, not helpful."

"We can't help that," Michael said. "We're just kids."

"Kids?"

"Children," Michael said. "Not grown up yet. Still learning."

"We had known you are immature specimens of your type. Are you not born with the knowledge of your parents?"

"No," my brother said. "You mean you *are?*"

There was silence for a long time. Michael had gotten the Twister to reveal something about his own race, something he hadn't intended to say. So they didn't know everything, and they weren't perfect. They could make mistakes. It was a good thing to know; a small victory, but I glowed inside with it.

"Our development is not of concern. Your intrusion upon us is."

"We didn't mean to intrude," Gemma said. "We were just trying to get *home.*"

"That will not be possible. You must stay here. We must consider what to do with you. You will now return to the small room."

"Wait a minute," I said. "We had a deal."

"What is a deal?"

"We answered your questions, now you answer ours."

A few seconds of silence, then, "Proceed."

A sigh of resignation would have fit perfectly in that pause. I had to warn myself not to fill in the clues I couldn't get from the faceless, voiceless Slarn from my own imagination. I had to keep telling myself this was an *alien* talking through a machine. If it even had emotions, they might not even be recognizable to an earthling.

In this situation, I couldn't tell if it was acting from a sense of honor, was just humoring me, or didn't care enough to mind if I wasted his time. All I knew for sure was that he had told me to proceed with questions, a situation I had better take advantage of while I had the chance.

"Where do you come from?" I demanded. "Why are you here?"

"There is no sound for the symbol of our planet's identity, or for that of our star. To us they are—" Here he did another couple of quick tentacle dances. "Our star system is in the central disk of this galaxy. Our planet circles a hotter star than yours, but at a greater distance; our planet is much like yours in size, mass, water-to-land ratio, atmosphere, and biology. We can breathe the air of Earth, eat its food."

Out of the corner of my eye, I saw Michael give me a sly "okay" sign, congratulating me again on my guess about their star. Twisters weren't the only ones who could communicate by gestures.

"What are you doing on Earth?"

"We have come to prepare the chronic discontinuity. The planet at present is too hot for our liking; we must take it over at a time when the temperatures are cooler."

77

Gemma was getting mad. "Why pick on our planet? We never did anything to you!"

"The assertion is nonsensical. You could not possibly have done anything to us. Even countless years in this planet's future, the time we must enter, you have made only the smallest beginning of space flight; you know nothing of the vibratory manipulation of space time."

"Then why don't you leave us alone?" she demanded.

"We cannot. We must have a new home. Earth is most suitable. Your kind must be removed so we can live here."

"But why?" Michael said. It wasn't just a protest; he really wanted to know.

Again, a pause into which a sigh would have fit nicely. "I will try to explain."

And to be fair, he did.

It took a while. The hardest part was at the beginning, when he tried to get us to understand what heroes he and his companions were.

The thing was, the Twisters here on Earth weren't an official invasion force. That is, they weren't sent by the government of their planet to conquer earth. They were a splinter group, a tiny minority of their people—Slarn told us fewer than two million—who saw themselves as pioneers yearning for freedom.

Their home planet, he explained, held a civilization that was already old, even now in the deep prehistory of the earth. They had learned how to recognize and subtly manipulate the energy vibrations that were the very fabric of space time; the setup we saw here was very primitive, clumsy vibration generators powered with the insufferably inefficient radiant energy of the sun. Still, that was the best they could do, and it would be enough. They would make it be enough. The home planet—he would wave his tentacles in the dance that meant the planet's name every time he made the machine mention it—he assured us, possessed wonders far beyond our imagining, let alone our understanding.

I didn't have any trouble believing that.

Unfortunately (he went on), all that learning and power had done nothing to bring about wisdom. War, crime, and pollution were rampant on the Twisters' planet, and the inevitable doubling of the population every seventeen star cycles led to overcrowding and made all these problems worse. An all-powerful dictatorship that restricted every phase of life held these terrors at bay.

But he and his companions in this mission were sick of the mess on the planet, and even sicker of the dictatorship. They had decided to find a new place to live.

And Earth was what they had found. Not the Earth we had stumbled into, 150 million years before our time, but the Earth we had left back in Marsdentown. A place with temperate climates, where the natives had already done much to enrich the land, and had mined natural resources and used them in such a way that they would be easy to reclaim.

"What does he mean by that?" I whispered to Michael.

He whispered back, "He means when we're all dead, if they want steel, they can just melt down a car instead of digging iron out of the ground.

I set my teeth, so it would be harder for any words to get past them. I didn't want to cut off Slarn now, though he might not have heard me even if I shouted. The news was grim, and the voice in which we heard the news was still rasping and harsh, but Slarn himself

79

was swaying back and forth, dancing his tentacles across the keys. He looked like a cross between a palm tree moving with a summer breeze and a great pianist being swept away by the beauty of his music.

In fact, he said as much. "The beauty of it. Two million of us, with a planet all for our own."

"We'll fight back," I said.

"That has been allowed for."

I was about to lose my temper. "You smug—"

Gemma cut me off. "Why Marsdentown?" she asked softly.

"You have used a sound symbol that has no meaning."

"Our town—the part of Earth where the time warp—your chronic discontinuity—has appeared is called Marsdentown."

"That part of Earth's surface is a place near the intersection of the vibratory planes of five of the seven major dimensions. It is there that the chronic discontinuity could most easily be created and sustained. We have been engaged in preliminary testing. Even now my companions are taking readings to ascertain the best place to open the actual gateway. I should be with them. We have no time to waste."

Slarn went on to outline the actual plan. Marsdentown was not only built at what was apparently the crossroads of the universe, it was isolated enough in Earth terms so that some kind of weird catastrophe—a stampede of dinosaurs sent forward from the Jurassic period, for instance—would empty the town long enough for them to transport their heavy-duty weapons to our time, and get on with wiping us out. Soon, he said, they would have perfected the technology to make the more difficult past-to-future transfer permanent, so that things sent in that direction remained there, rather than snapping back to their own time. That solved the mystery of the stegosaurus tracks.

"But something is going wrong."

Good, I thought.

"Some external vibration is causing a small rip in the fabric of space time in an undesired place. You have discovered us. I must learn what that vibration is; it may be vital to our sustaining the large-scale discontinuity we must achieve to fulfill our plan."

He wasn't swaying to his beautiful scenario of a nearly empty Earth populated by animated palm trees. He was stiff and rigid (except for the tentacles—they were never still), almost like a statue.

"Have I answered your questions?"

"All but one," I said.

"Ask it."

"What happens to us?"

"You need not die."

I'm ashamed to say this, but my heart leapt when I heard the words. Why I would want to go on living with the rest of the human race served up as dinosaur chow or worse is beyond me, but I wasn't thinking logically at the time.

Anyway, my elation only lasted a second, because Slarn went on, "My knowledge of your planet is still imperfect. Though as ... 'kids' ... you lack the full knowledge of your race, you know much that can be useful. How your kind will react to the stimuli of fear. How best to exploit the resources left behind. Your youth could be an advantage to us. You can then render long service and live out your natural life span."

I was so mad I was almost sick. "You mean, all we have to do is betray the human race to you, and you'll let us live?"

"You have used a sound symbol that has no—"

"Don't pretend you don't know what 'betray' means! If you've got wars and crime on your planet, you know what treachery means just as well as any human does. And just in case you don't, it means to turn against those who ought to be able to trust you!"

"The concept is indeed known. The sound symbol was not."

"Yeah, well let me use it in a sentence for you, then. None of us will *ever* betray the human race to a bunch of lime-eyed monsters. You don't even—"

Again, Gemma spoke quietly. "I'll help you," she said.

My jaw almost bounced off the floor. I grabbed her by the shoulders and spun her around. "Gem!" What's the matter with you?"

"I don't want to die, Jon."

Burning tears blinded me. By the time I'd wiped them away, Slarn had made his machine say, "You are wise. Wait here. I will give these others a chance to reconsider."

He came out from the round keyboard and wrapped tentacles around Michael and me. I fought harder than I'd ever fought before. I even bit him. Michael had been right. He tasted terrible, and it did no good.

Holding us in two tentacles, he used a third to get the sonic gizmo that opened the door, made it do its stuff, then threw us into the small room and closed the door again.

I just lay where I landed and cried.

I hadn't cried like that since I was younger than Michael. I cried until I thought my lungs were going to rip, and my eyes felt so hot I thought they were going to melt and get washed out of my head by my tears.

After a while, Michael lay down beside me, put his mouth near my ear, and said in a harsh whisper, "Don't you think you're laying it on a little thick?"

"What do you mean?" I said between sobs.

"I think you've got them convinced you're upset," he whispered again.

"Upset?" I screamed. "I wish I was dead."

Still whispering, Michael put a hand on my shoulder and said, "Okay, okay. Keep your voice down. Didn't you see what Gemma did?"

I was still screaming. "Of *course*—"

"Shhh!"

"Of course I saw what she did," I hissed. "She sold out me, you, our parents, every human being on Earth."

"No she didn't, you dope. It's a fake."

"A fake?"

For the first time since we'd come back into the room, I glanced at Michael's face. He looked really disgusted with me.

"Yeah," he said, "a fake. Didn't you see her wink at you?"

I was stunned. I hadn't. I told Michael.

"She did it as soon as you swung her around," he informed me. "I don't see how you missed it."

"I missed it," I said, "because I started crying as soon as I heard her say she'd help them."

Michael made a noise with his mouth. "Boy, what a stinky friend you are. I thought you were faking the hysterics to help Gemma convince Slarn you thought she really meant it. I thought it was a good idea, so I went into hysterics, too. For your sake, we'll just leave it that way, okay?"

I snuffled a few times, wiped my nose, and went to get up. "No," I whispered. "If I ever get the chance I'll apologize."

"That'll take guts."

"I'll find some," I promised. "Somewhere. Michael?"

"Yes, Jon?"

"Why are we whispering?"

"In case they have the room bugged. They can hear and understand English, remember, even if they can't talk."

"Oh, right," I said. "But won't Slarn get suddenly suspicious if we spend the whole time in here whispering?"

"Probably. That's why you should get up and we should talk about what a rat Gemma is."

So we did that for a while. It wasn't easy, now that I knew what a heroine she was being, spying on the Twisters. Who knew what they'd do if they caught her? I was glad Michael had straightened me out, but it would have been easier to put on our show if he hadn't.

Fake talk about what a louse Gemma turned out to be flowed naturally into real talk about what stinkers the Twisters were.

Michael could really get into that one. "Why didn't they just ask Earth for help? With their super science, they could have helped us out a lot, and got rich themselves. There'd be room for them, even two million."

"They don't *want* to be made room for. They want all the room for themselves," I said. "Besides, I don't think they have a lot of respect for us."

"Yeah," Michael said. He thought for a while. "You know, what they're planning to do to Earth is what Europeans did in North and South America and in Africa."

"Hah!" History was the one subject I could go toe-to-toe with Michael on. "Europeans did some terrible things, all right, and exploited the people who were already living there like mad. But what they didn't do was go in deciding ahead of time they were going to *slaughter every last one of them.* That's what the Twisters have planned for all of us—everybody, all over the world."

"Good point," Michael said.

Somehow, it failed to cheer me up.

We were mostly silent for the next couple of hours, except for times when one of us would think of something we'd like to do to the Twisters, the more gruesome the better.

Then the door opened and Gemma walked in.

My first impulse was to run to her and give her a big hug, but I remembered in time that I was supposed to hate her guts, so I turned my back on her and walked to the far wall.

She stood there, kind of embarrassed—until the door closed. Then she said, "Guys, I think we can get out of here."

"Quiet," we said, "they may be listening!"

"They're not. That was one of the first things I found out. Since they don't talk among themselves, they never think of listening in, that's my theory. There's a TV camera in here, or something that works like one, at least, but they can't read our body language. Slarn kept asking me what you two were up to. I told him you were in despair, and only needed some convincing to come over to his side. That's what I'm doing here. I've got overnight to convince you, then—" She drew a finger across her throat.

Michael, as always, went right to the most important thing. "You said we can get out of here? How?"

"It's simple," she said. "That thing he tucks in his bark or skin or whatever it is. It makes a three-note harmonic, in thirds."

"That's simple, huh?" I said.

"After eight years of piano lessons, it sure is. One of the reasons I faked wanting to help them was to learn the chord for the outer door. It turns out to be the same one. The sound things are like keys, see. On their home planet, it probably works fine because—"

"Because they can't make any noise!" I realized. It was nice to have beaten Michael to it. The rest of it was coming to me, too. Gemma had perfect pitch, and was a trained musician. She must have figured out the right notes by now.

I turned to my brother. He looked glum.

"Michael, don't you get it? All we have to do is each

of us whistle the note Gemma tells us, and the door will open.''

"I know that,'' he said, sounding miserable. "I just don't know if I can.''

"You can whistle. I've heard you whistling. One day you went around whistling 'Yankee Doodle' until I thought you were going to drive me nuts.''

Michael looked helpless. " 'Yankee Doodle' is all I *can* whistle.''

"Oh,'' I said. I couldn't think of much else to say.

"It's all right,'' Gemma said. "We'll work this out somehow. Michael, whistle 'Yankee Doodle' for me.''

"Right now?'' Michael asked meekly.

"No, squirt, on the Fourth of July. Of *course* right now. We ought to wait a while before we open the door, give Slarn a chance to go out and join his pals in their vibration hunt—he was really eager to do that; I think it was one of the reasons he wanted me in here with you guys. He doesn't trust me, no matter what I said. But we ought to make sure we can get out of here as soon as we can.''

That made sense. My brother puckered up and blew a breathy version of Yankee Doodle. It wasn't great, but you could recognize it.

Gemma had a look of patient thoughtfulness on her face. She wasn't ordinarily the patient type. This made her look very grown up, like a teacher.

"That was terrific,'' she said, "but a little too high.'' She whistled a note. "Start there.''

Michael couldn't match the note, even after hearing it ten times.

Gemma was great with him. She didn't get excited,

she just tried something else. "Okay," she said, "whistle it along with me. Try to make the same notes I do."

That, Michael could do. He whistled it through with a great feeling of relief. Being as smart as he is, he's not used to running into things that he can't get right off.

They whistled it together a few times. The next time, after the first couple of notes, Gemma stopped, and Michael went on and did it himself. They did it that way again, and he was fine. But when she asked Michael to do it himself from the start, he went back to the higher note again.

"It doesn't matter," Gemma said. "When the time comes, I'll start you off."

"I'm sorry I'm not getting it right."

"Don't be silly," she said. "You're doing fine. Now, one more thing, and we're set."

Michael got nervous again. "One more thing?"

"Yeah, it's simple. I don't want you to whistle the whole thing through. I want you to stop with the first note of 'riding' and just sustain it."

"You mean keep whistling the same note?"

"Yeah. Not over and over, though. I want you to draw it out. Like this." She whistled it for him.

I had a suggestion. "Think of the words as you do it," I told him. " 'Yankee Doodle came to town, a-riiiiiiiiiii,' like that."

He looked doubtful. "I'll try," he said.

"Okay," Gemma said, "start with me," and she whistled the first couple of notes, then let him go. He did fine; at least Gemma said so. He didn't sustain the note very long, it seemed to me, but I wasn't the expert.

Next, Gemma taught me my note. I'm a pretty good

whistler, so I was able to do it to her satisfaction after only three or four tries.

By now, enough time had gone by for us to try the door.

We walked up close to it. It was so tight with tension that I was afraid my muscles were going to snap my bones. What if this didn't work? What if it had been a trick, and the Twisters were on the other side waiting to get us?

I looked at my watch. It would be close to dinnertime back on earth. That was all the more reason for us to get out of here, and not because I was hungry, either. I had thought of something.

I couldn't believe how calm Gemma's voice was.

"Okay," she said, "let's give it a try. Michael, with me."

They began to whistle together, Gemma dropped out, Michael went on. ". . . came to town a-riiii . . ."

I added my note, a lower one, and Gemma added one above. It sure sounded like the sound Slarn's gadget made.

The door thought so, too. It began to slide open.

It opened six inches worth, then Michael lost the note, and it slammed shut.

"Oh, *rats!*" Michael said. "I blew it. I mean, I didn't blow it. I mean, I'm sorry."

"Stop apologizing," Gemma told him sternly. "Take some big breaths before we start again, stock up on oxygen. Then just hold the note longer this time."

Michael gave a solemn nod, and we began again.

This time, I leaned right up against the wall next to the door, but I didn't watch the door, I watched my brother. When he got to the right note Gemma and I joined in, and just like last time, the door began to slide open. Michael did better; it was a good five seconds longer before he showed signs of running out of breath. As soon as I saw them, I turned to the door. It was open about a foot and a half. I jumped into the gap.

I realized as I did it that I had no idea how powerful that door was. I could be jumping into something that would cut me in half lengthwise.

Too late now. I put my back against the doorjamb and my hands and feet against the edge of the door.

Well, it didn't cut me in half, but it was a heck of a tight squeeze. I pushed with all my might, but the door was going to win.

"Come on!" I grunted. "Squeeze . . . through."

I think I mentioned somewhere earlier that these were the two smartest kids I knew, and they proved it again this time, doing things exactly right.

For instance, Gemma went first. Why? Because that opening was created by my strength, and it was obvious it was only going to get smaller, so the bigger kid should go out first. Also, if only one of them could get out, Gemma should be the one, so she could give a rap to Slarn when he got back.

It seemed to take forever, though it probably wasn't more than a few seconds. Gemma was out, then she reached back and pulled Michael through the ever-dwindling space between me and the door like the first pickle out of the bottle.

Just when I figured my back was going to bust, he was free. All I had to worry about now was myself.

There was nothing dignified about the way I jumped clear of that door, lurching violently to get my body clear, then pulling my legs to me like a frog to get them away from the door's final snap.

As I lay on the floor catching my breath, Gemma and Michael gathered around telling me what a great job I did.

"Thanks," I said, "but let's look around and find something to prop the next one open with, okay?"

We did so, while I kept checking my watch. We had time not only to do that, but something else as well.

"Before we go," I said, "let's leave them something to remember us by."

"What do you mean?" Gemma said.

"Let's bust up the place. Set their project back so Earth has a little breathing space."

Gemma was horrified. "Jon!" she said. "We can't do that! If we smash the thing that makes their vibrations, or whatever it is, we'll never get home."

I hadn't thought of that. Now we faced a horrible decision. What was more important, to hinder the Twisters, or to warn people back in Marsdentown, and the whole world we grew up in?

You don't know how glad I am we never had to answer it.

"Don't worry," Michael said. "Look, this thing that's humming is obviously the vibration generator, and these wires to the roof lead to the antennae up there. This square thing it's attached to is obviously a battery. That makes sense. Solar energy is only available half the day, so you need a battery for the rest of the time. All this other stuff"—he indicated bunches of machinery—"is solar power collection equipment. If we smash that, the generator should be kept running until the battery runs out."

"Michael," I said, "are you sure of this?"

"I'm mostly sure. I mean, the technology may be different, but the laws of physics have to be the same."

I looked at Gemma. "I think we have to risk it," I said.

She gulped. "I can't believe I'm saying this, but I agree with you." She turned to Michael. "You'd better be right, squirt."

"I'll be punished enough if I'm wrong," he said, which was absolutely true.

Anyway, we found a couple of metal rods sheathed in plastic, about five feet long, and as big around as a kielbasa. And we began to smash everything Michael told us it was safe to smash.

Now, ordinarily, I've got no use for vandals. People like my mom work hard to build things, or to pay for them, and people who go around ruining things with bricks and paint cans are just jerks as far as I'm concerned.

But having said that, I have to say this—busting up that place was *fun*. Considering that we were maybe saving the lives of everyone on Earth, and especially in our hometown, the crunch and tinkle of things breaking was like music.

Finally, we were done. I brought a suitable chunk of debris with me over to the door, put it down, and checked my watch.

"Why do you keep doing that?" Michael demanded.

"Doing what?"

"Looking at your watch."

"I want to know what time it is."

"Well," he said, "that won't do you any good."

"Sure it will. It's running, see?" I held it out for him to see the sweep hand move.

"But that's not the time *here*," he protested. "It's the time back home."

"I know that. The time back home is what I'm interested in. If we can manage it, I want to get to the place of the time warp just after dinnertime back in Marsdentown."

Now Gemma was interested. "Why?" she asked.

"Because I'm pretty sure that's when the hole is going to open up again."

"You are, huh?"

"Yup," I said. "I've figured out what's causing the time warp."

TWELVE

Whatever time it was back (or forward, I guess) in Marsdentown, it was just about noontime here. Once outside the door, we blinked in the sunlight and looked at each other.

The thing was, we had spent so much of our energy working on getting out of the Twisters' blockhouse that we forgot to make a plan about what to do after we escaped.

We decided that the simplest solution was best—we'd just make a beeline for the place we'd come through. It should be easy enough to spot the place in daylight. We'd kept the steel-and-plastic rods with us, for aid in walking, and for protection.

"Yeah," Michael said, "but what do we do if they spot us again?"

"We know what to look for now," I pointed out. "We won't let them surround us this time."

"And they can't move very fast," Gemma said. "We should be able to outrun them."

We started off, checking frequently to make sure we had the mountain at our backs. We got maybe five hundred yards past the bottom of the hill when I looked back and saw a Twister on the crest. He started waving his tentacles in a mad, four-armed semaphore.

"Let's move," I said. "We've been seen. He's signaling the others about us."

"I wonder how they get each other's attention."

"I don't know, but I don't think he's doing that for fun, and I don't want to hang around to ask him."

"Good point," Michael said.

I wasn't too worried. As we'd said before, now that we knew what they looked like, they were too darn big to sneak up on us, and they didn't move very fast, either.

Then Gemma pointed back at the hill. "Look what he's doing!" she said.

Turned out the Twisters had two ways of traveling. There was the way we'd seen, swinging the tentacles and inching forward on the "stumps," and there was this. The Twister had thrown itself full length on the ground, and was crawling like a snake, as well as pulling itself along with big, swimming motions of its tentacles.

"Moves a lot faster that way," Michael reflected.

"So should we," Gemma said.

We ran through the jungle, not worrying too much about picking our way, just crashing through, vines, prickers, and all. We used the rods we'd stolen to smash or lever branches out of our way. We could hear the distant thrashing of Twisters behind us; they made even more noise this way.

We stayed well ahead of them, until we came to a swamp.

It wasn't that we minded the swamp. Since we'd gotten here, we'd been through so many swamps we practically knew the prehistoric dragonflies by name. It was what was going on at that particular swamp.

A stegosaurus, much bigger than the baby who'd bitten me (maybe this was its mother), was mired at the far edge of the swamp, with its spiked tail tangled in a big clump of half-rotted vegetation, so it couldn't be used to defend itself.

What it needed to defend itself from was a pack of four or five nasty critters about five and a half feet tall that looked like skinny, half-grown allosauruses. Every time the stegosaurus would try to get out of the muck, these guys would rush forward and nip at its legs and side. When the stegosaurus tried to snap at them to keep them away, they went for its neck.

I looked at my watch. If my theory was right, we didn't have time to go far enough out of our way to avoid this mess.

"Come on," I said. "Maybe they won't notice us." They certainly seemed busy enough with the stegosaurus. We quickly made it around the edge of the bog.

They noticed us. There were five of them. Three kept after the stegosaurus while the other two turned to face us. Both of them had enough sharp teeth for five or six dogs and sharp, curved claws. They stood there looking at us with beady little black eyes.

"What do you call these, Michael?" Gemma asked.

"I think these are ornitholestes."

I gripped my rod like a baseball bat, ready to strike. "How long are they going to stand there like that?"

"Until they think they can get us."

That made sense. It also made sense that the thrashing of the Twisters through the brush was getting larger and closer. It was an angry sound.

It seemed like a choice between being recaptured by the Twisters and being chopped up by these animated lawn mowers.

Suddenly, Gemma said, "Oh, the *heck* with it!" With a loud, wordless battle cry, she rushed forward, waving her rod over her head.

Sometimes, all things take is courage. Gemma bonked the lead ornitholestes on the head with her rod; it let out a squeal like a punished puppy, and ran off into the woods. A couple of pokes and prods by Michael and me on the other, and it was gone, too.

Not a moment too soon, either. I could see tentacles flailing at the edge of the bog. I started to rush on, but Michael said, "Wait!" and ran to attack the three who were bothering the stegosaurus.

I had nothing against stegosauruses, even though I was the only human ever to have been bitten by one. But since they were already extinct, I didn't exactly feel an obligation to save this one. However, I couldn't let my baby brother rush into those teeth all alone. Gemma and I joined in, and the nasty bullies were soon gone.

"Can we go now?" I demanded.

"Not yet," my brother said. "Let the stegosaurus get out of the swamp first."

"The Twisters are almost here," Gemma pointed out. "If we wait here, we'll be caught!"

"If we don't," Michael retorted, "we'll be caught about two hundred yards farther on. Trust me."

We didn't have a lot of choice. One of the Twisters was already on the far side of the bog. He stopped there, bending his trunk in the middle to raise his eyes to a position from which they could see us.

Meanwhile, the stegosaurus had been pulling itself

slowly out of the bog. It took its own sweet time about it, too.

Even Michael was beginning to worry. "Come on," he urged. "I know you can do it."

It finally did, but not before the first Twister had already made it halfway around the edge of the bog toward us, and three more had appeared on the far side.

As soon as the stegosaurus was free, Michael shouted, "Now!" and clambered up its broad hips, using the plates along its spine as handholds. Gemma caught on immediately, and was right behind him. I hesitated a few seconds and had to run a bit to catch up with the creature before scrambling up the other side.

That turned out to be a good thing. After being mired in the swamp for so long, the stegosaurus wanted to stretch its legs a little. That suited us fine, because the Twisters were right on us. As I climbed up the side of the dinosaur, I felt the tip of a tentacle grab for my ankle, but I pulled free just in time.

The stegosaurus would certainly carry us free of the Twisters—if it would keep moving at top speed, which it seemed to want to. The only trouble was, it didn't necessarily want to go in the direction we wanted it to.

That was another problem Michael solved. A tap with one of the rods on the side of the stegosaurus's neck would keep it from turning. With alternate taps from the two of them on the left side and me on the right, we managed to keep it reasonably straight.

The Twisters were falling behind, but they didn't give up. They were still land-swimming in our wake, and somehow, I knew they wouldn't stop, even at the edge of the Jurassic period. To protect their plan, they would follow right through the time warp, if it was open, and kill us and everybody else who happened to see them.

"Listen," I yelled through the plates on our steed's back, "when we get there, you two are going to have to wait just inside the time warp and hold them off for a minute or so. I've got to do something." They didn't ask how they were supposed to hold them off with nothing but a couple of plastic-coated metal rods, which was good, because I didn't know.

Gemma had something else on her mind. "What makes you think the time warp is going to be open?"

"Because at home it's just after dinnertime," I said, "and my mother is very predictable."

There was no time for further talk, because there we were. Our basement was just a dark, irregular oval hanging in the bright jungle daylight, but if you squinted, you could make out the washer and the dryer in there.

"Yippee!" Michael said.

Then we learned something we hadn't thought of earlier. There is no way to make a dinosaur "whoa." It kept stampeding, thundering on. For a second, I thought it was going to try to cram itself right through the time warp, but it began to veer aside. I threw my rod away, yelled, "Jump!" and flung myself through the air. I don't think I needed to yell. By the time I rolled over and got to my feet, Michael and Gemma had already landed. Since they were on the other side of the mount, they were closer to the warp than I was.

It was touching to see them ignore the gateway home to come and see how I was, but it was also irritating. "Get through the warp!" I told them.

"Not without you," Gemma said.

"It won't be without me," I promised. We ran for

the warp, holding hands. I had twisted my ankle on landing, and it hurt, but it did *not* slow me down. When we got through the opening, and felt the gritty concrete floor of the cellar under our feet, it was almost possible to believe the whole thing had been some kind of hallucination—until you looked back, and saw the Twisters' relentless advance on us.

"I'll be back in a minute," I promised. "Slow them down."

I bolted for the cellar steps. Behind me, Michael and Gemma were piling junk in front of the opening to make an obstacle course for the Twisters.

As I climbed the steps, I heard the familiar rumble and whine of the malfunctioning dishwasher.

Because that was the key. The whole thing was based on vibrations, and a new, weird, unplanned-for vibration had torn open that hole in time and space. In our basement.

And where did we find new, weird, and unplanned-for vibrations? In our dishwasher.

I burst through the cellar door into the kitchen.

Mom was sitting at the kitchen table with Gemma's parents, drinking coffee. Their eyes were red from crying. Gemma's father knocked his cup over and didn't even move while the hot liquid soaked his pants.

Mom was the first to find her voice; she *is* a lawyer, after all.

"Jon!" she yelled. "Where have you—"

"In a minute, Mom," I said.

I rushed to the dishwasher, and threw the lever that shut it off. I ran back to the cellar door, and yelled down the stairs.

"Everything okay?"

"Fine," they called back. They were walking toward the stairs to join us. "Warp closed. What did you do?"

"I'm not through doing it."

"Jonathan Parlo, I insist you tell me—"

I was back at the dishwasher. I knelt in front of it, and opened the door. I reached under the bottom rack through the water at the bottom, to the drain circle.

My fingers grabbed something hard and metallic, and I pulled it out and looked at it and laughed.

I turned around to find my mother glaring at me. Michael had come to my side.

"We sure missed you, Mom," he said. He *is* a genius. Mom's face fell into tears, and filthy and wet as we were, she wrapped us up in a big hug. It felt good. Across the room, Gemma was being enveloped by her parents.

When we came up for air, I held up the thing I'd pulled out of the dishwasher. It was a little gold star, on a dangle, attached to a clasp.

"Here, Mom," I said proudly. "I found your earring."

THIRTEEN

So that's how we saved the world.

Think about it. If Mom's earring hadn't fallen into the dishwasher and prematurely opened the gateway to the Jurassic, the Twisters would have been able to flood us with dinosaurs that following summer, establishing a beachhead for their invasion.

As it was, we managed to throw a big monkey wrench into their plans.

Not that our troubles were over, by any means. For one thing, we had to explain why we were missing for thirty-six hours. Michael started to blurt out the truth, but all it got him was a bunch of dirty looks and the possibility of a spanking.

From the point of view of what we first intended to go back for, that is to find proof that we had dinosaurs in our basement, our mission was a big failure. It might have been the coward's way out, but neither Gemma nor I backed up Michael's story.

Instead, she came up with a doozy of her own. According to her, we had gone out early Saturday morning to see Jupiter move across Orion, or something like that. We were out on the front lawn when some men in ski masks came by in a van and stuffed us in. We were locked in a dirt-floored garage by them, while they went on some other mysterious errand.

This appealed to Michael. "Yeah," he said eagerly. "The leader's name was Twister Slarn."

My mother looked at him, but Gemma plowed on. We managed to escape from the garage by digging dirt away from the opening, but we had to leave our coats behind. We were lost in the woods for most of the day, but finally we found the stream that flows at the rear of our property, and we followed that back. We came in through the basement window because we wanted to scout out the situation first, and find out maybe if he hadn't come back here.

Michael's next suggestion was better. "We thought it might have something to do with one of your cases, Mom."

Mom looked thoughtful.

"Jon," she said, "why did you run right to the dishwasher?"

My turn to fib now. "Um," I said, "ah, because when I heard the dishwasher going, I knew that nobody was in here holding you hostage. You wouldn't run the dishwasher at a time like that."

It turned out she wouldn't have run it at all except that she'd about run out of coffee cups. That's all she and Gemma's folks had done since the Davises had rushed back from their convention once they'd learned we were gone. They didn't eat, they didn't sleep, they just sat there and drank coffee and worried about us. I was touched. I was also glad she'd run out of cups when she had, because if she hadn't we almost certainly would have been recaptured.

"And when I thought about the dishwasher, it came

to me in a flash where your earring had gone to, and I know how much it means to you, so I wanted to get it."

But even that wasn't the end of it. There were cops and doctors and people who wanted us to "own our fear," whatever that means. The fear wasn't about what we'd said it was, but we were the sole proprietors of it. We were just glad it was over with.

Back at school, we got a little added respect as kids who had outwitted kidnappers, but mostly, it was no big deal, since aside from scrapes and bruises, we hadn't been hurt.

But there's another bit of fear the three of us own. That's the fear that the Twisters aren't going to give up. I can still see Slarn swaying at that keyboard as he talked about how wonderful it would be to have the planet for him and his two million pals to play with. And I shudder a little.

And since no grownups and darned few kids will listen, there was only one thing I could think of to do.

I wrote this book. Gemma's father is going to see if he can help me get it published. He thinks it's a good joke—he even liked it when I told him what this ending was going to say. If it gets published, it'll go as a story, with made-up names in it, but at least it will accomplish this: If the Twisters try again, at least all the known facts about them will be available to anybody who wants them.

In the meantime, one genius, one real smart kid, and one ordinary one will be working hard to think of ways to defeat them.

And you, reading this book, even if you think it's all pretend, why don't you work on the problem, too?

Next time, it may be you who saves the Earth.

Join in the Wild and Crazy Adventures with Some Trouble-Making Plants

by Nancy McArthur

THE PLANT THAT ATE DIRTY SOCKS
75493-2/ $3.99 US/ $5.50 Can

**THE RETURN OF THE PLANT
THAT ATE DIRTY SOCKS**
75873-3/ $3.99 US/ $5.50 Can

**THE ESCAPE OF THE PLANT
THAT ATE DIRTY SOCKS**
76756-2/ $3.50 US/ $4.25 Can

**THE SECRET OF THE PLANT
THAT ATE DIRTY SOCKS**
76757-0/ $3.50 US/ $4.50 Can

**MORE ADVENTURES OF THE PLANT
THAT ATE DIRTY SOCKS**
77663-4/ $3.50 US/ $4.50 Can

Coming Soon
**THE PLANT THAT ATE DIRTY SOCKS
GOES UP IN SPACE**
77664-2/ $3.99 US/ $4.99 Can

IF YOU DARE TO BE SCARED...
READ SPINETINGLERS!
by M.T. COFFIN

(#1) THE SUBSTITUTE CREATURE
77829-7/$3.50 US/$4.50 Can

No one believes Jace's crazy story about seeing the new substitute, Mr. Hiss, in the men's room...smearing blood all over his hands and face!

(#2) BILLY BAKER'S DOG WON'T STAY BURIED
77742-8/$3.50 US/$4.50 Can

Billy Baker's dog Howard has come back from the dead...bringing all his friends from the pet cemetery.

(#3) MY TEACHER'S A BUG
77785-1/$3.50 US/$4.50 Can

(#4) WHERE HAVE ALL THE PARENTS GONE?
78117-4/$3.50 US/$4.50 Can

(#5) CHECK IT OUT—AND DIE!
78116-6/$3.50 US/$4.50 Can

LOOK FOR THESE OTHER TERRIFYING TALES COMING SOON

(#6) SIMON SAYS, "CROAK!"
78232-4/$3.50 US/$4.50 Can